KB067511

대니

〈K-픽션〉 시리즈는 한국문학의 젊은 상상력입니다. 최근 발표된 가장 우수하고 흥미로운 작품을 엄선하여 출간하는 〈K-픽션〉은 한국문학의 생생한 현장을 국내외 독자들과 실시간으로 공유하고자 기획되었습니다. 〈바이링궐 에디션 한국 대표 소설〉 시리즈를 통해 검증된 탁월한 번역진이 참여하여 원작의 재미와 품격을 최대한 살린 〈K-픽션〉 시리즈는 매 계절마다 새로운 작품을 선보입니다.

The 〈K-Fiction〉 Series represents the brightest of young imaginative voices in contemporary Korean fiction. This series consists of a wide range of outstanding contemporary Korean short stories that the editorial board of *ASIA* carefully selects each season. These stories are then translated by professional Korean literature translators, all of whom take special care to faithfully convey the pieces' original tones and grace. We hope that, each and every season, these exceptional young Korean voices will delight and challenge all of you, our treasured readers both here and abroad.

대니
Danny

윤이형 | 전승희 옮김
Written by Yun I-hyeong
Translated by Jeon Seung-hee

K

ASIA
PUBLISHERS

Contents

대니
Danny

기름기가 동동 뜬 뜨거운 믹스커피 속에 얼음덩어리 몇 개가 녹으며 돌고 있었다. 달고 뜨겁고 찬 커피를 들이켜자 관자놀이께가 얼얼했다. 한 모금 겨우 마시고 나는 잔을 내려놓았다.

그럼, 시작해볼까요.

최 형사가 리모컨을 집어 들었다.

말투를 주의해서 들어보세요. 사용하는 단어들 같은 거요. 음성은 다르지만 잡아낼 만한 특징이 있을 겁니다.

나는 고개를 끄덕였다. 불이 꺼지고, 눈앞에 걸린 커다란 스크린에 영상이 재생되기 시작했다.

나란히 앉은 젊은 부부가 카메라를 응시한다. 삼십대

A few ice cubes were floating around and melt-
ing on the hot, grease-floating, mixed coffee.
Drinking this sweet, hot, and cold coffee, I felt a
smarting pain in my temples. After barely a sip, I
put the cup down.

Let's start, then.

Detective Choe picked up the remote.

Listen carefully to the way they speak. Their vo-
cabulary, for example. Although the voices are different, you could probably pick up on their individual characteristics.

I nodded. The light was turned off, and the
screen in the front of the room began to repro-

초반쯤 됐을까. 동안으로 보이지만 남자와 여자는 내 예상보다는 나이가 많을 것 같다. 피어싱을 한 것도 머리를 분홍색으로 물들인 것도 아니고, 철없는 짓을 벌일 것 같지도 않다. 남자는 얌전해 보이는 안경을 썼다. 여자는 눈이 토끼처럼 동그랗다. 단아한 흰색과 베이지색 위주의 옷차림에, 둘만 집에 있어도 조곤조곤 존댓말로 대화할 것 같은 인상이다. 프레임 밖에서, 질문이 시작된다.

질문: 그날 여기 이분, 이 할머니를 봤을 때, 무슨 생각을 하셨다고 했죠?

여자: 음……. 힘들겠다, 힘드시겠다 하는 생각? 실은 동네에서 오며 가며 많이 뵌 분이었거든요. 그쪽에선 저를 모르시겠지만. 보면 항상 어린 아기, 손주를 데리고 계셨는데, 몸이 좀 불편해 보이셨어요. 제가 친정엄마가 안 계시거든요. 그래선지 돌아가신 친정엄마 생각도 나고, 좀…… 도와드리고 싶다는 생각도 들었고.

질문: 그래서 도와드리려고 말을 걸었나요?

여자: 음, 꼭 뭘 구체적으로 도와드리려고 한 건 아니고요.

duce large images.

A young couple, sitting next to each other. They stare at the camera. Perhaps early thirties? Although their faces look young, they might be older than I guess. No piercings or dyed, pink hair is visible. They don't look as if they'd act childishly. The man wears modest-looking glasses. The woman has round eyes like a rabbit's. They wear elegant white and beige clothes. They look like they'd speak softly with each other and use high forms of speech even when they're alone at home. The first question begins outside of the frame.

Q: That day, what did you say you thought when you saw this, this elderly lady, here?

Woman: Mmm... I think I thought that it must be hard, hard for her. I had actually seen her in the neighborhood before then from time to time. Though I don't think she knew me. She would always have a baby, her grandson, with her, but she never looked well. I lost my mother, you know... Maybe because of that, I thought of my mother when I saw her. So... I felt like helping her.

Q: Did you talk to her to help her?

Woman: Mmm... I did not mean to offer her any

질문: 그러면요?

남자: 음, 저기요. 사람이, 그냥 말 한번 걸어보고 싶을 때도 있잖아요. 동네에서 자주 뵙는 할머닌데. 꼭 이유가 있어야 되는 건 아니잖습니까.

질문: 알겠습니다. 그런데 왜 다른 때, 직접 얼굴을 대하고가 아니라 그런 특수한 방법으로 말을 걸고 싶으셨을까요? 그것도 그런 단어를 사용해서요.

남자: …….

여자: …….

질문: 거기다가, 그때 두 분의 따님인 지희 양이 놀이터에서 놀고 있었단 말이에요. 아이에게 집중해야 하는 상황이었는데 왜 그런 행동을 하셨죠?

여자: 심심해서요.

남자: 여보.

여자: 가만있어봐요. 사실 그대로만 말하면 되잖아. 잘못한 것도 없는데.

질문: 심심하셨다고요?

여자: 저, 죄송한데요, 질문하시는 분은 혹시 아이 있으세요? 네 살짜리 아이가 놀이터에서 놀 때 한 시간이고 두 시간이고 뒤 졸졸 따라다니면서 아무것도 못하고

concrete sort of help.

Q: Then what?

Man: Um, so, you know, we all have times when we feel like talking to someone. Since we saw her in the neighborhood often, we didn't feel like we ever needed to have any reason to talk to her, y' know?

Q: Okay. So, then, why did you want to talk to her in such a specific way, and not face to face when you saw her? Especially, using that word?

The man and woman are silent for a while.

Q: Besides, your daughter Jihi was playing in the playground. You had to pay attention to your daughter. So, why did you do that?

Woman: I was bored.

Man: Honey.

Woman: Don't. We just have to tell them the truth, right? We did nothing wrong. So....

Q: You were bored?

Woman: Well, I'm sorry, but do you have any children? When you have to follow your child around all day while he runs around on a play-ground for hours on end and just watch them be-

지켜보는 거, 그거 하루도 빠짐없이 하면 굉장히 지루하거든요.

질문: 그런가요.

남자: 수퍼바이징 모드일 때는 우리가 걱정할 일이, 없었어요. 대니가 워낙 아이를 잘 봐주다 보니까.

여자: 그때가 오후 네 시쯤이었나 그럴 거예요. 회사 일은 대충 정리된 시간이었고, 노파심으로 접속해서 애를 보긴 보는데, 정말 신경을 안 써도 될 정도였어요. 그러다 보니 그 상태로 다른 사람들도 보고, 딴생각도 조금씩 하고, 그렇게 되던데요. 다른 부모들은 욕할지도 모르겠지만. 아마 욕을 하겠죠. 근데 글쎄요, 저희는 그랬네요.

남자: 사람들이 서로 얘기할 때도, 그냥 오로지 얘기만 하지는 않잖아요? 보통은 폰을 보든지, 딴걸 하면서 얘기를 하잖아요.

질문: 알겠습니다. 굉장히 지루하고 심심해서, 그래서 이분한테 말을 거신 거군요.

여자: 대니가 되어보고 싶기도 했던 것 같아요.

남자: 여보.

여자: ……아주 잠깐요. 그냥 장난이었어요. 그래요,

cause you know you're not supposed to do anything else, if you do that day after day, you get
really bored, y'know.

Q: Is that so?

Man: When it was in supervising mode, we didn't
have to worry... at all. Danny was really good at
babysitting.

Woman: I think it was around four in the afternoon. We were pretty much done with our busi-
ness, and although we kept an eye on our daughter just to make sure, we really didn't have to worry
at all. So we looked at other people, thought of
other things, that was just natural, y'know? I guess
some parents might criticize us. They probably already do. At any rate, that's how we were.

Man: When people talk with each other, you
know, they don't just talk, right? Usually, they look
at their phones, or do something else while they're
talking.

Q: Okay, so you were just very bored and so you
talked to this lady.

Woman: I think I probably wanted to become
Danny, too.

Man: Honey.

Woman: (after a pause) Just for a very short mo-

좋은 장난은 아니죠. 근데 사이버공간에서도 다들 아바타를 쓰지 않나요. 그게 그렇게 큰 잘못인가요? 그냥 그 할머니를 쳐다보는데, 내가 이 할머니라면 어떨까 싶었어요. 내가 이 할머니인데, 대니같이 생긴 남자애가 와서 말을 걸어주면 기분이 어떨까. 기운이 좀 나지 않을까? 그래서 대니인 척해본 거예요. 충동적으로요. 그렇지만 딱 한 번이었고, 그날 이후로 저희는 그분한테 말을 걸지 않았어요. 블랙박스를 열어보시면 나올 거예요, 아마.

질문: 알겠습니다.

화면이 멈추고, 불이 켜졌다.

차가운 물 한 잔이 추가로 내 앞에 놓였다. 내 낯빛 때문인 듯했다. 내가 물을 다 마시기를 기다려 최 형사가 물었다.

어떠세요? 생각나시는 게 좀 있나요?

어떤가? 나는 자신에게 물어보았다.

그러고는 생각을 거듭한 끝에 겨우 대답했다. 잘 모르겠다고. 최 형사가 거의 들리지 않는 소리로 한숨을 쉬었다. 방 안에 있던 다른 사람들도 조금씩 지친 표정이

ment. It was just a prank. Yes, that's right. It wasn't a good prank. But everyone uses an avatar at some point, right? Is that such a crime? I was just—I was just looking at her and thought: What would it be like if I had been her? If a boy like Danny came and talked to her, what would she feel? Wouldn't she feel invigorated? So I pretended to be Danny. It was just an impulsive thing to do. But that was the only time. We haven't talked to her since. You can check the black box and confirm, I think.

Q: I see.

The screen stopped and the light came on.

They put one more cup of cold water in front of me. Because of my face, perhaps. After I finished drinking the water, Detective Choe asked me.

What do you think? Can you remember anything?

What do I think? I asked myself.

Then, after thinking long and hard, I said finally that I couldn't say. Detective Choe sighed almost inaudibly, but I still heard it. The other people in the room seemed tired as well.

Shall we listen again from the beginning? Or would you like to watch another interview? We have an interview tape with the couple's daughter.

었다. 처음부터 다시 한 번 들어볼까요? 아니면 다른 인터뷰를 볼까요? 두 사람 딸 인터뷰도 있는데 그것부터 보시겠어요?

……그리고 그 비슷한 제안과 질문 들, 인터뷰 영상 들. 방 안을 채우고 있던 여러 명의 사람들. 언어학자, 심리상담가, 범죄학자, 변호사, 기계생명공학자, 정부 기관에서 나온 사람들. 그렇게 많은 전문가들과 이야기를 나눈 일은 내 인생에 처음이었다. 아마 마지막이기도 할 것이다. 다시 커피 한 잔, 질문과 대답. 다시 제안, 차가운 물 한 잔 더. 다시……. 그런 일들이 그날의 나머지 시간 내내 계속되었다. 민우를 안은 채 울상을 짓고 있던 딸아이와, 연신 담배를 피우러 드나들던 사위의 지친 얼굴이 떠오른다.

그날 나는 옆에 있던 조금 작은 방에서 마지막으로 대니를 만났고, 그 뒤로 다시 그를 보지 못했다.

이것이 내가 갖게 되어 있는, 그가 등장하는 기억의 마지막일 것이다. 막다른 골목. 수술칼로 깨끗하게 자른 것 같은, 아무것도 개입할 여지가 없는 서사의 끝.

그러나 내게는 다른 기억이 있다.

Would you like to watch that first?

And then similar proposals and questions, inter-view screens. Many people came and went in the room. Linguists, clinical psychologists, lawyers, mechanical biotech engineers, governmental offi-cials. That was my first time talking with so many people. And most likely my last time. Another cup of coffee, questions and answers. Another sugges-tion, another cup of cold water. And again and again like that. It lasted the remainder of the day. I remember my daughter, her face crumpled and about to cry, Minu in her arms and my son-in-law looking tired, coming in and out of the room to smoke.

I met Danny for the last time that day in a smaller room next door; I haven't seen him since.

This was the last of my memories of him, memo-ries I was supposed to have. A dead end. The end of a narrative, one not to be intervened with, as if cleanly cut with a surgical knife.

But I have another memory.

*

The summer I met Danny, I was sixty-nine. Suf-

*

　대니를 만난 여름, 나는 예순아홉 살이었다. 그해 여름엔 비가 많이 내렸고 슬개골연골연화증을 앓고 있던 나는 통증을 잊기 위해 종종 콧노래를 흥얼거리곤 했다. 대니는 스물네 살이었고, 탄탄한 팔다리와 아이들의 사랑을 독차지하는 재주, 영원히 늙지 않는 심장을 지니고 있었다.

　대니가 내게 마지막으로 한 말이 무엇이었는지는 생각나지 않는다. 아마도 별 특징 없는 말이었던 모양이다. 마지막이 언제였고 어떤 모양이었는지도 사실은 흐릿하다. 하지만 그가 처음으로 내게 건넨 말은 다른 것과 혼동할 일이 없다. 그건 네 음절로 된 단어였다.

　아름다워.

　그 말을 얼핏 들었을 때 나는 놀이터에 있었다. 민우를 유모차에 태우고 막 버클을 채우려던 참이었다.

　아이가 허리를 비틀고 발을 구르며 날카로운 소리로 짜증을 뱉어냈다. 가만있어, 할머니 힘들다. 많이 놀았지? 이제 집에 가는 거야. 타이르며 서둘러 허리를 펴는

fering from chondromalacia, I often hummed a song in order to forget my pain. Danny was twenty-four, and had strong limbs, a talent for acquiring the absolute love of children, and a heart never to grow old.

I cannot remember what his last words to me were. They were probably something ordinary. In fact, I'm not even that sure when was the last time I saw him and how he looked. Yet I am not confused about what he said to me first time. It was a three-syllable word:

Beautiful.

When I first overheard that word, I was at the playground. I was about to buckle Minu in the stroller where I had just put him.

Minu was struggling against me, turning his body, stamping his feet, and shrieking. Stay still, you make it hard for me. Didn't you play enough? Let's go home now. After admonishing him like that, I stood up and I couldn't help moaning in pain. I checked to see if Minu was sitting comfortably, held the stroller handle with both hands, and released the brake. It was only then that I realized

데 끙, 소리가 입에서 절로 나왔다. 아이가 제대로 앉은 걸 확인하고 유모차 핸들을 두 손에 쥐고 브레이크를 풀었다. 좀 전에 누가 뭐라고 하지 않았나 싶어 고개를 돌린 건 그다음이었다.

물 빠진 노란색 티셔츠를 입고, 청바지에 운동화를 신은 젊은 남자가 이쪽을 보고 있었다. 눈이 마주치자 그가 웃었다. 확인하듯, 그가 다시 말했다.

아름다워요. 정말로.

남자의 피부는 지나치게 희었고 눈과 입은 좀 어색하다 싶을 만큼 컸다. 특히 까만 눈은 내가 본 적 없는 거대한 열대 과일에서 떨어져 나온 씨앗 같았고, 구불구불한 머리카락은 커다란 검은 물고기의 몸에서 뜯어낸 비늘처럼 보였다.

가스불 중불 정도 크기로 마음속에서 경계심이 켜졌다. 저 남자는 나를 보고 왜 저렇게 웃는가. 천지 구분 못 하고 뛰어다니는 말만 한 중고등학교 애들까지만 해도 아직 사람이 덜된 보송한 어린것이라는 생각이 들어 괜찮았다. 하지만 그보다 위, 이십대나 삼십대들의 환한 웃음을 보면 나는 이유 없이 시선이 떨궈지고 잘못한 것도 없이 주눅이 들었다. 주름도, 상처도, 나쁜 의도

that someone had said something a little while ago, and so I turned around.

A young man, wearing faded yellow T-shirt, jeans, and sneakers, was looking at me. When our eyes met, he smiled. Then, he repeated himself as if to make sure I heard it.

Beautiful. Really.

His skin was a little too pale, and his eyes and mouth were rather large, almost awkwardly so. His dark eyes, especially, stood out like large black seeds that had fallen out of a giant tropical fruit I had never seen before. His curly hair looked like scales that had been taken out of a large black fish.

In my heart, my sense of wariness grew to the size of a medium gas light. Why was he smiling at me like that? Teenagers mindlessly horsing around in their adult bodies seemed harmless to me. They were unripe children, not yet full-grown human beings. But when I saw the bright smiles on the face of men in their twenties or thirties, I couldn't look straight at them for some reason and I lost my heart from no fault of mine. Faces without wrinkles, scars, or ill will, faces that hadn't broken or collapsed. Those faces, hanging in the air like blades of light, trembled absentmindedly. I kept on

도 없고 아직 부서지지도 무너지지도 않은 얼굴들. 그
얼굴들은 빛으로 만든 칼날들처럼 허공에 걸려 무심하
게 흔들렸다. 멀리서는 봐도 가까이 다가가진 않는 게
좋겠다는 생각이 자꾸 드는 건 아마도 무심히 상처 입
히는 능력을 잃어버린 자의 질투였을 것이다.

민우야, 고맙습니다 해. 아저씨가 칭찬하네.

아뇨, 저기, 당신이 아름답다고요.

누구, 나요?

네.

예에?

…….

아이구, 고마워라. 내가 오래 살아 젊은 사람한테 별
칭찬을 다 듣네.

서둘러 자리를 피할 요량으로 나는 다소 과장된 웃음
을 지었다. 무해한 농담에 공연히 날을 세울 필요는 없
었다. 남자는 부모 중 한쪽이 한국인이 아닌 듯했다. 외
모도 그랬지만 구사하는 한국어도 다소 어색했다. 그의
얼굴에 걸린 웃음이 조금씩 줄어들더니 미소가 되어 멎
었다.

몇 개월이에요?

thinking that I could observe them from afar, but I shouldn't go near them, probably because I felt jealous of them; I had lost the ability to hurt others absentmindedly.

Minu, say, "thank you." That uncle is saying nice things about you.

No, I mean, I think you're beautiful.

Who, me?

Yes.

Really?

He didn't respond.

My, thank you. I've lived so long that now I even see the day a young man compliments me.

In order to escape this scene with the young man, I exaggerated laughing. I didn't have to be all nerves at a harmless joke. From his looks, one of his parents must not have been Korean. Not only was his appearance somewhat exotic, but also his Korean was a bit awkward. His bright smile gradually reduced in size and eventually shrank to a faint smile.

How many months old is he?

Oh, my grandson? His first birthday was a few months ago, so, he's fifteen months old now.

Oh, that's quite a difficult time.

우리 손주요? 지지난달에 돌 지나고, 보자, 이제 15개월이네.

아아, 한창 힘드시겠다.

그러게. 요것이 요즘에 땡깡이 늘어가지고 조금 힘드네. 근데 힘든 걸 어떻게 아나?

저도 조카를 봐주고 있거든요. 저기 있는 저희 조카는 지금 36개월 8일 됐어요.

36개월하고, 8일? 정확도 하다. 참 꼼꼼한 삼촌을 뒀네.

사람들이 그러던데요. 자식을 키우는 엄마는 강해야 하지만 손주를 키우는 할머니는 강하고 인자하고 명랑하기까지 해야 한다고. 삼촌은, 음, 그런 건 없네요.

그가 웃었다. 힘드시죠? 그래도 힘내세요.

땀이 스며 나온 얼굴이 따가웠다. 간장처럼 짠 햇빛이 쏟아졌다. 항의나 추궁, 변명이 아닌 내용으로 낯선 사람과 그만큼 오래 대화한 건 몇 년 만의 일이었는데 나는 자꾸만 졸아붙는 느낌이었다.

샴촌! 대니 샴촌! 멀리서 여자애 하나가 소리치며 뛰어왔다. 흰 원피스를 입고 머리를 양 갈래로 묶은 까만 얼굴의 여자애였다. 아이는 순식간에 벤치 위로 뛰어올라 남자의 등에 올라타고는 목을 조르며 악을 써댔다.

That's right. He's been throwing quite a few tan-trums these days, making it a little hard for me. But how do you know that?

I, too, am taking care of my niece. There, that girl is my niece, thirty-six months and eight days old.

Thirty-six months and eight days old? How exact you are! A very attentive uncle you must be.

People told me that a mother should be strong, and a grandmother should be strong, benign, and even cheerful, but an uncle, well, doesn't have such requirements.

He laughed. It's hard, isn't it? But stay strong!

My face was stinging from sweat. Sunlight, as salty as soy sauce, poured down. It had been a few years since I'd last talked with a stranger about something that wasn't a protest, an accusation, or an apology. For some reason, I felt like shrinking away.

Yuncle! Yuncle Danny! A girl was running to-wards him. The girl had a dark face, pigtail braids, and was wearing a white dress. The next moment the girl jumped up on the bench. Then she launched herself onto his back, choking him around the neck and yelling. "Gyo! Danny! Gyo! Robot! Stand up! Stan' dup! Go, go! Go, go, go!

가쟈! 대니! 가쟈! 로봇아! 일어나! 스탠 덥! 고고! 고고 고! 남자가 행복해죽겠다는 표정으로 엉거주춤 일어나 아이를 지탱했다. 나는 목례를 하고 놀이터를 나와 집 으로 가는 언덕길로 유모차를 밀기 시작했다.

올드타운으로 이사 왔을 때 나는 내 집의 싼 방세와, 그에 어울리게도 동네의 다른 모든 것들이 폭 낡았다는 사실에 감사하는 편이었다. 있을 것들은 다 있었다. 제 법 큰 전통시장, 오래된 떡집과 작은 빵집 들, 사우나와 찜질방, 산에서 나물거리를 캐다 길에서 파는 여자들, 옛날식 놀이터와 공원, 등산로까지. 오래된 삶의 방식 을 보존할 목적으로 시에서 세피아벨트를 둘러 지정해 놓은 이 지역은 타임캡슐에서 빠져나온 듯한, 노인들이 살기에는 최적의 조건을 갖춘 동네였다. 딱 한 가지가 문제였다. 내가 사는 건물에는 엘리베이터가 없었다. 매일 집으로 돌아오는 길에 언덕을 오르며 무덤들처럼 꾸역꾸역 붙어 선 케케묵은 건물들, 반세기쯤 전에 지 어진 듯한 빌라들을 볼 때마다 나는 계단을 오를 생각 에 다리가 후들거리고 가슴이 턱턱 막히곤 했다.

사이비 종교 권유라도 하려는 거였을까. 아니면 그냥

The man got up halfway, his face overjoyed, and balanced the girl carefully. I nodded, left the playground, and began pushing the stroller over the hill towards my house.

When I moved to this old town, I felt rather grateful for the cheap rent and, fittingly, the pretty, worn-out things all over the neighborhood. There were still all the things there that anybody would need: a decent-sized, traditional market, an old rice cake shop, small bakeries, a sauna, and a *jjim-jilbang*. There were women selling vegetables they had picked on the mountains, an old-fashioned playground and park, and even hiking paths. This neighborhood, a sepia-belt designated for the purpose of preserving an old-fashioned lifestyle, was one best suited for the elderly. It was as if it had just emerged from a time capsule. There was only one problem. There was no elevator in the building I lived in. Every day on my way on the hill to my house, looking at the crowded, outmoded buildings that stood huddled throughout the town, like graves, townhouses built half a century ago, I felt breathless and my legs shook.

Was he trying to talk me into joining a cult? Or

삶이 무료한 사내였나. 문득 조금 전 남자와 대화할 때의 내 목소리가 떠올랐다. 깨진 기왓장을 어디 대고 탁, 탁 두드리는 듯 물기 없이 흙 부스러기가 날리는 음성이었다. 나는 내 목소리가 갑자기 낯설게 느껴졌고 마음에 들지 않았다. 아무도 강요하지 않았는데 어디선가 스스로 주워 와 입에 붙어버린 노인 특유의 성조(聲調)도 마찬가지였다.

마음에 안 들면 뭘 어째. 실없는 웃음이 나왔다. 번쩍 안아 올려 아기띠에 옮겨 담자 울상이 된 아이가 허리를 활처럼 뒤로 휘며 몸부림치기 시작했다. 집에 들어가기 싫어 튀어 나가려는 11킬로그램짜리 아이를 캥거루 새끼처럼 앞에 매달고 5.7킬로그램 나가는 유모차를 접어 한 팔에 들었다. 민우는 쉬지 않고 구슬눈물을 흘리며 악을 질러댔다. 5층까지 올라가는 동안 너무 힘들어 두 번 쉬었다. 마지막 반 층을 올라갈 때는 속옷이 조금 젖고 말았다.

그날 밤은 유달리 어려웠다. 하다 하다 안 돼서 딸아이를 호출해 홀로그램 통화까지 했는데도 민우는 계속 울었다. 들쳐 업고 자장가를 부르며 시커먼 방 안을 뱅글뱅글 돌다 포기하고 자리에 누웠다. 아이는 두 시간

was he someone simply bored? I could hear my own voice talking to the man a while ago. It was a dry voice, a sound that a broken roof tile would make when it was struck on something and had begun breaking and crumbling. Suddenly, my voice felt strange to me, and I didn't like it. I didn't like its tone either, a tone typical of an old lady, a tone that nobody had forced on me, but that I had somehow picked up.

So I don't like my voice, so what? I smiled, feeling silly. When I picked up my grandson and put him in the baby carrier, he made a face that looked like he was about to cry. He began to struggle, bending his body backward like a bow. Supporting an eleven-kilogram baby struggling to spring away in front of me like a baby kangaroo, I folded the 5.7-kilogram stroller and carried it in one arm. Fat tears continued to roll down Minu's cheeks. It was so hard to climb up to the fifth floor that I had to take a break twice. On the last flight of stairs, I ended up slightly wetting my underwear.

It was a particularly difficult night. Eventually, I even called my daughter through the hologram-projector and had Minu talk with her. But Minu kept crying. I piggybacked him and sung him a lul-

반이 지나서야 울다 지쳐 잠들었다. 가녀린 목에 흘러
내린 침을 닦아주다 나도 기절하듯 까무룩 잠이 드는
와중에, 낮에 들은 말이 꿈결 속으로 스며들었다.

아름다워요. 정말로.

*

다른 피해자들 증언은 완료됐죠?

네, 적게는 백만 원에서 많게는 천만 원까지 요구했다
고 합니다. 블랙박스 자료에 의하면 첫 만남에서 두번
째 만남 정도를 빼고는 수퍼바이징 상태에서 사용자가
대화를 직접 입력한 기록은 없다는 게 공통점이고요.

거짓말 탐지기 분석은 끝났습니까?

네. 해당 사항 없다고 나왔습니다.

그렇다면 AI에서 자의적으로 생성해낸 반응 패턴이
라는 말이군요. 그런 일이 가능한가요?

이 모델에 탑재된 AI 버전이 4.65예요. 인간 감정의
80퍼센트를 느끼고 재현할 수 있고, 중간 정도 수준의
농담을 할 수 있고, 질문에 대답하지 않고 침묵을 선택
할 수도 있죠. 하지만 '금품 갈취' 같은 건 당연하게도,

laby. I circled inside a darkened room and then finally gave up and lay down. Minu cried himself to sleep two and half hours later. I fell asleep as if I were fainting, wiping the saliva from Minu's slender neck as I eventually lost consciousness. Just before I fell asleep, I could hear the words I had heard during the day seep into my dream.

Beautiful. Really.

*

Done with other victims' testimonies, correct?

Yes, they said that they received demands to pay one to ten million *won*. According to the black box data, except for the first and second meetings, there was commonly no record that showed the user input dialogues directly in the supervising mode. Have they completed the lie detector analysis?

Yes, it proved irrelevant.

Then it means that that was a response pattern that was voluntarily produced in the AI. Is that possible?

The AI version loaded in this model is 4.65. It can feel and reproduce 80 percent of human emotions,

할 수 없어요. 돌보미형으로 특화되어 있기도 하고, 인간의 도덕에 비춰 문제가 되는 패턴은 만들어지는 것 자체가 불가능하니까요. 그런데 모르는 사람에게 돈을 요구하고 협박하는 게 아니라 친구에게 돈을 빌린다, 이런 패턴이라면 가능할 수도 있어요, 이론적으로는.

친구요?

네. 혹은 그만큼 친밀한 관계로 인식이 된다면요.

그 정도로 막역한 관계를 스스로 만들 수 있다는 건가요?

그보다는, 어떤 패턴을 이끌어내는 걸 목표로 설정해두고 사용자가 첫 만남에서 대상을 고의적으로 메모리에 강렬하게 각인시켰을 수 있어요. 그럴 경우 사용자 개입이 다시 이뤄지지 않아도 AI 자체 내에서 반응 트리가 그쪽 방향으로 생성될 가능성이 있죠. 말하자면 사람들이 많이 다니는 대로변에 난데없이 집채만 한 바위 하나를 뚝 떨어뜨려놓는 것과 비슷해요. 그러면 그 주위에 자연히 사람들이 몰려들고, 바위에 대한 이야기가 오가고, 바위를 치워야 하지 않겠느냐는 쪽으로 의견이 모아지고, 결국에는 치워지거든요. AI의 논리회로에도 별로 어렵지 않게 같은 일이 일어나게 할 수 있지

present a moderate degree of levity, and choose to remain silent instead of answering a question. But, naturally, it can't perform actions such as "extortion by threats." It's specialized as a caretaker type, and also it's fundamentally impossible to create a pattern built on questionable human morality. Not to extort a stranger, but to borrow money from a friend—a pattern like that is possible, at least theoretically.

A friend?

Yes, or someone close to being a friend.

It can voluntarily create that kind of a close relationship?

Not that, but the user could have intentionally etched someone deeply in its memory in its first meeting in order to induce a certain pattern. In such cases, even if the user wasn't interfering with it again, one could generate a response tree in that direction within the AI. In other words, it's like you drop a giant, house-sized rock along a crowded main road all of a sudden. People will naturally crowd around the rock, talk about it, conclude that they should remove it, and then, eventually, actually remove it. It's not particularly difficult to make the same thing happen within the logic circuits of

요. 마음만 먹는다면.

　정황이 상당히 미심쩍군요.

　네, 피해자들이 모두 육십대에서 칠십대 사이, 혼자 아기를 키우는 노인들이라는 점도 마음에 걸립니다. 하지만 사용자의 고의라는 물적 증거가 없어요. 그냥 버그일 가능성도 배제할 수 없죠.

　그럼 일단 반품 처리해서 분석하게 되나요?

　네. 아무래도 예전 그 일도 있었던 데다, 꽤 민감한 사안이라서요. 오늘 중으로 전량 회수에 들어가게 될 것 같습니다. 이후에는 연구개발팀으로 넘어갑니다.

　　　　　　　　　　　*

　아이는 아름다웠다. 곱고 사랑스럽고 반짝반짝 빛났다. 내 핏줄이 뻗어간 가지 끝에 이런 것이 맺혀 있다니, 믿을 수 없을 정도로 감사하고 뭉클한 존재였다. 흩날리는 벚꽃잎 같고, 밤새 쌓인 첫눈 같았다. 세상에 하나뿐인 보석들만 모아 정성껏 세공해서 만든 귀한 그릇 같기도 했다.

　그 빛나는 그릇에 매일같이 담기는 타는 듯이 뜨겁고

an AI. If only you mean to do it.

The circumstances are quite suspicious.

Yes, it bothers me that all the victims are between the ages of sixty and seventy, and all elderly
women raising children alone. But there is no
physical evidence that suggests that it was the result of user intention. We cannot rule out the possibility that this was just a bug.

Then are we just to recall them all and analyze
them?

Yes, since there was that precedent, and this is
quite a sensitive subject, you know. It seems that
we'll have to recall all of them today. After that we'll
send them to the R&D department.

*

The baby was beautiful. Pretty, lovely, and brilliant. How this beautiful thing could have sprouted
from the last branch of my bloodline! The baby
was a being for which I was unbelievably grateful
and which moved me deeply. It was like cherry
blossoms falling and flying, like the first snow that
fell and accumulated overnight. It was also like a
precious, gem-studded bowl with each gem carefully chosen.

검은 약을 남기지 않고 받아마시는 것이 내 일이었다.

어느 날 집 앞 교회 바자회에서 김치를 사 왔다고 했더니 딸아이가 대뜸 물었다. 엄마, 그 김치 몇 킬로야? 10킬로? 10킬로를 쓰러지지 않고 들고 다닐 수 있다는 거야? 그럼 엄마, 우리 민우 봐줄 수 있겠네. 내가 복직을 해야 빚을 갚지. 이대로는 도저히 숨도 못 쉬겠고 정말 죽을 것 같아.

나는 노인복지센터에서 마련해준 일자리를 그만두고 싶지 않았다. 지역 도서관에서 카드를 순서대로 정리하거나 홍보 책자를 종이봉투에 넣고 봉하는 일차원적인 노동이었고 벌이도 적었지만, 내겐 그냥 하찮지만은 않은 일이었다. 나는 유유자적 시장을 구경하거나 산바람 강바람을 쐬고 싶을 때 적적하게나마 산책할 자유를 포기하고 싶지도 않았다. 그러나 성치 못한 무릎 정도로는 거절할 핑계가 되지 못했다. 고관절염이나 동맥경화 같은 병명들을 매달고 중환자실에 누워 있거나 지팡이를 짚고 팔자걸음을 하는 노인들에 비하면 나는 대단히 건강한 편이었으니까. 사위는 고등학교 때 부모를 한날한시에 사고로 잃고 혼자 자란 처지였고, 딸아이 입장에선 내가 유일하게 비빌 언덕이었다.

Drinking up the hot and black herb tea that filled that shining bowl everyday was my job.

One day, when I said I bought *kimchi* at the church bazaar in front of my house, my daughter immediately asked: Mom, how heavy is that *kimchi*? 10 kilograms? You can carry 10 kilograms without collapsing? Then, Mom, I think you can take care of my Minu. I need to go back to my work to pay off my debts. I can't even breathe living like this. I think I'm really dying.

I did not want to quit the job I had gotten through the elderly welfare center. Although it was one-dimensional work, like cataloguing and stuffing envelopes with fliers in the neighborhood library, and it didn't pay much, it was not such trivial work to me. I also didn't want to give up my freedom of leisurely strolling in the marketplace, or taking solitary walks when I felt like fresh air. But my bruised, tired knees weren't excuses enough to refuse my daughter's request. In comparison to the old people who lay in intensive care units, with coxitis or sclerosis, or those who walked with their toes turned out and only with the help of canes, you might consider me really healthy. My son-in-law grew up alone after losing both his parents

출산하고 6개월이 지나자 딸은 복직을 했고 나는 민우를 맡았다. 한 달에 백만 원 조금 못 되는 생활비를 받아 분유와 기저귀를 사고 고기와 야채죽을 끓였다. 딸아이는 주말마다 민우를 데리러 와 눈물을 글썽이다가도 월요일 아침 도로 데려다 놓고 갈 때는 뒤도 돌아보지 않았다.

새벽 6시쯤부터 자정까지 나는 집 안에서 서서 일했다. 생각할 겨를 없이 그저 반사적으로 몸을 움직이면 아이의 요구를 겨우 반 정도는 채워줄 수 있었다. 민우는 잘 먹고 잔병치레 없는 아이였으나 순한 아이는 아니었다. 쉬지 않고 돌고래처럼 악을 썼고, 원하는 게 있으면 손에 들어올 때까지 발을 구르고 물건을 집어던지며 울었다.

나는 기계가 아니다.

집이 비는 주말이면 나는 가게에서 소주를 사다 한 병씩 마시며 그렇게 중얼거렸다. 중얼거린 다음에는 차라리 기계라면 좋겠다는 생각이 들었다. 몸이란 건 웃기고 요망한 덩어리라 음식물처럼 혼자만의 시간도 주기적으로 넣어줘야 제대로 일을 하겠다고 우아를 떨어댔다. 평소에는 내가 그저 기름 약간 거죽 약간을 발라

overnight from an accident when he was a high-school student. So my daughter had only me to fall back on.

Six months after giving birth, my daughter went back to her work, and I began taking care of Minu. I bought powdered milk and diapers and boiled meat and vegetable soup with an allowance of less than a million *won* a month. My daughter came to me tearfully every weekend to pick up Minu, but she didn't even turn back when she left him after dropping him off every Monday morning.

From six in the morning until midnight, I worked on my feet. If I didn't think at all and simply responded to the baby's demands, I could barely fulfill half of the baby's demands. Minu ate well and didn't get sick often, but he wasn't an easy baby. He cried incessantly, piping and squealing like a dolphin. When he wanted something he would throw a tantrum until he got it, stamping his feet and throwing things until I relented.

I'm not a machine.

I muttered this while sipping on a bottle of *soju* that I bought from a neighborhood store on the weekends, when I was finally alone. Those times, I really did wish I were a machine. The human body

놓은 뼈 무더기 같다가도, 조용한 방에 앉아 컵에 따른 소주를 천천히 목으로 넘기고 있으면 그나마 사람이라는 더 높은 존재로 회복되는 기분이었다. 가끔 검푸른 한강물 생각이 났다. 천사 같은 손주 키우기가 유일한 소일거리이자 낙인 늙은이, 그게 내게 주어진 역할이었다. 아무도 내가 울 만큼 힘들 수도 있다는 걸 알지 못했다.

아이 혼자 키우기는 젊은 시절 이미 한 번 넘어본 산이었다. 그러나 그때는 젊음 특유의 회복력과 반드시 더 나은 날이 오리라는 대책 없이 질기고 바보스러운 기대, 그리고 어찌 됐든 이건 내가 선택한 길이라는 쇳덩어리 같은 각오 들이 하루의 틈마다 빼곡히 들어차 있어 앞이 안 보이는 전쟁통에도 넘어지지 않을 수 있었다는 걸 나는 뒤늦게 깨달았다. 이제 내겐 그런 게 없었다. 이런 것을 생존이나 생활이 아니라 삶이라 부를 수 있는 것인지도 확실치 않았다. 나는 일종의 숟가락 같은 것으로 변해 있었다. 나는 휘청이는 몸에 위태롭게 아이를 얹고 낮에서 밤으로, 하루에서 다른 하루로 끝없이 옮겨놓을 뿐이었다.

is a strange thing. It puts on airs, claiming that it can work only when it's regularly provided with alone time for itself, like it claims it needs food. Although I might be just a heap of old bones covered over with a few drops of oil and a several patches of skin, I felt as if I had recovered my higher being as a human being when I sat alone in my quiet room and slowly passed *soju* from my cup to my throat. Sometimes I thought of the deep blue of the Han River. A senior woman whose only pastime and recreation was the angelic task of raising her grandson—that was the role assigned to me. Nobody knew that it was so hard for me that I couldn't help crying sometimes.

Raising a baby alone was the mountain I had already climbed up and down when I was young. I belatedly realized that I could stand straight without falling down on that unpredictable, warlike journey only because I filled every minute of every day of it with things like the youthful ability to recover, the helplessly persistent and idiotic expectations of a better day, and an ironclad resolution to follow through with what I had chosen to do in my life. I didn't have these things any more. I wasn't sure whether a life like that could be called life, not

유제품 진열대에 붙어 있던 거울이 기억난다. 탈모가 반쯤 진행된 내 회색 머리카락은 반송장이라는 말이 딱 일 지경으로 산발이었다. 늘 입는 갈색 몸뻬바지 위에 진홍색 스판 티셔츠를 걸치고 나는 땀을 줄줄 흘리며 서 있었다. 그러다 그와 눈이 마주쳤다. 그는 거울 속 조금 떨어진 뒤쪽에서 나를 보고 있었다.

마흔 이후로는 거울을 신경 쓰지 않고 살았다. 어느 날 마주 본 거울이 텅 비어 있었다 한들 별로 놀라지 않았을 것이다. 노화해가는 육체를 의지대로 통제할 수 없게 된 지 오래라는 사실이 내 추레함에 당위를 부여해주었다. 나는 아무거나 집어먹고 손에 닿는 대로 대충 입으며 살고 있었다. 그러나 그날 그와 나를 함께 비추던 그 거울이 나를 놀라게 했다. 거울은 그런 몰골을 한 내가 허깨비가 아니라 진짜 사람이고, 다른 사람의 눈에도 비치는 존재이며, 따라서 자신의 모습에 책임을 져야 한다고 알려주었다.

이리 주세요. 제가 옮겨드릴게요.

아니, 괜찮아요.

그러지 말고 주세요, 저한테.

저기, 왜, 왜 그래요?

just subsistence or survival. I had become a sort of utensil, like a spoon. I loaded the baby precariously onto my swaying body and carried it from day to night, from one day to the next.

I remember the mirror attached to the dairy product display stand. My thinning gray hair was so disheveled that I would fit the phrase "a half-dead person." Wearing my usual loose-fitting trousers and crimson spandex T-shirt, I realized I was sweating like a pig. It was then that I exchanged glances with him. He was looking at me in the mirror from a little behind.

I had lived without paying attention to a mirror since the age of forty. I wouldn't have been much surprised to find the inside of a mirror I happened to look into empty. The fact that I could no longer control my aging body according to my will justified my shabbiness to me. I ate whatever fell into my lap and I wore whatever clothes I could lay my hands on. But that mirror that reflected my image back to me surprised me that day. It let me know that my form and shape was no phantom, but a real flesh-and-blood human being that could be reflected into someone else's pupils, and that I had to

네?

학생인가? 나 알아요?

아, 지난번에 놀이터에서, 만났는데.

아니, 근데, 괜찮다는데 왜 그러느냐고요. 내 짐 내가
들고 간다는데?

결국 길 한복판에서 나는 소리를 질렀다. 목소리에 유
리 조각이 섞여 나왔다. 북어 몇 마리, 부추와 파와 두부
를 사고 기저귀 한 팩을 손에 들었다. 그 정도면 무거운
짐은 아니었다.

놀이터에서 마주칠 때마다 웃어주는 것까지는 그러
려니 했다. 나나 아이나 하고 다니는 양을 보면 가계 사
정이 삐져나온 속옷마냥 빤하니 민우를 어떻게 하려는
건 아닐 거라고 나는 생각했다. 성도착자나 정신에 문
제 있는 사람처럼 보이지도 않았다. 웃는 걸 좋아하고,
사람을 좋아하는 무료한 청년. 그런데 그날 그는 슈퍼
마켓에서부터 강아지처럼 나를 졸졸 따라왔다.

왜 그렇게 짜증이 나는지 알 수 없었다. 순수한 친절
이자 호의에서 나온 듯 보이는 그의 살가운 태도가 몹
시도 견디기 어려웠다. 그것이 실은 내게 친절도 호의
도 베풀어주지 않는 타인들에 대한 짜증이라는 사실을

be responsible for my appearance.

Give it to me. I'll help you, ma'am.

No, that's okay.

Please, let me help you.

Well, why, why are you doing this?

Excuse me?

Are you a student? Do you know me?

Oh, I met you... in the playground the other day.

So I told you I'm fine, okay? I'm carrying my stuff myself, okay?

In the end, I had to yell at him in the middle of the road. My voice came out mixed with shards of glass. I was carrying a few dried pollacks, leaks, scallions, and tofu in one hand and a pack of diapers in the other. They weren't too heavy.

He smiled whenever we ran into in the playground, and that seemed harmless to me. He wouldn't have any intention of hurting Minu, given how clear our financial situation must have been. You could just tell by the way Minu and I looked. It was as clear as a pair of underwear peeking out. He didn't look like a pervert or psycho either. A bored young man who liked to smile and took to people easily. But, that day, he followed me like a puppy from the supermarket.

그 순간에는 알지 못했다.

　불편, 하신가요. 불편하게 해드렸다면 죄송합니다.

　그가 내 눈치를 살피며 중얼거리고는, 아기띠 속에서 잠든 민우를 보며 덧붙였다. 저는 해치지 않아요. 아기도, 당신도.

　해치지 않는다는 건 알겠는데.

　네.

　다른 사람의 감정도 조금은 읽을 줄 알아야지.

　…….

　남자가 말없이 고개를 숙였다. 민우가 게슴츠레 눈을 떴다. 아이 이마에 물방울이 떨어졌다. 회색 보도에 점점이 짙은 얼룩들이 번지기 시작했다. 어느 지붕 밑으로 피해야 하나 둘러보는데 남자가 한 손에 들고 있던 우산을 펼쳤다. 아주 큰 우산이었다.

　쏟아지는 장대비가 재미있는 모양이었다. 우유를 다 마신 민우가 창밖을 보고 꺄드득 소리를 내며 웃었다.

　빗줄기가 잦아들 때까지만 앉아 있기로 했다. 남자는 아무것도 주문하지 않았고, 나는 모과차를 시켰다. 방금 전까지 폭발할 것 같던 기분이 차 한 잔에 사르르 풀

I didn't know why I was so irritated. I couldn't stand his affectionate offer, something that probably originated from pure kindness and good will. I didn't realize at that moment that that irritation was in fact my irritation toward others who had never shown me any sort of kindness or good will.

Are you... uncomfortable? I'm sorry if I made you feel uncomfortable, ma'am.

He glanced at me, and then murmured, as he looked down at Minu asleep in the carrier, I don't harm your baby, or you.

I know you don't, but...

Yes?

You should try to read other people's feelings better.

He bowed silently. Minu opened his eyes a little. A water drop fell onto his forehead. Dark spots were spreading on the gray sidewalk. I was looking around to find an overhang where I could hide when the man opened an umbrella that he'd been carrying all along. It was a very large umbrella.

Minu must have found the downpour fun. After finishing his milk, he giggled loudly and stared out the window.

리는 게 어이없었고, 어린애에게 필요 이상으로 꼰대질을 한 것 같아 민망하기도 했다. 웃고 있는 민우를 보니 집에 돌아가면 빨래도 반찬도 관두고 이대로 하루 일과가 끝이었으면 싶었다.

혹시, 아세요?

오래 말이 없던 남자의 입에서 나온 건 뜻밖에도 옆 도시에서 일어난 킨더가든 참사 이야기였다. 비 오는 오후에 찻집에 앉아 나누기에 맞춤인 얘기는 아니었지만 나도 알기야 알았다. 보육 시설에서의 아동 학대와 폭행, 사망사건이야 옛날부터 비일비재했지만, 5년 전의 그 사건은 규모에서나 계획적 범죄였다는 점에서나 예전과는 구별될 수밖에 없었으니 말이다. 같은 친목 모임에 속해 있던 세 명의 킨더가든 보육 교사가 시간차를 두고 각자 다니던 직장에 불을 질렀고, 0세에서 4세 사이의 아이들 마흔두 명과 교사 여덟 명이 목숨을 잃었다.

범인들은 모두 잡혔으나 사건의 충격이 가라앉는 데는 상당한 시간이 걸렸고, 그 결과 전국 보육 시설 가운데 적지 않은 수가 사실상 폐원 상태에 들어가게 되었다. 가족이 아닌 남의 손에 아이를 맡기는 일은 정상적

I decided to stay in the tearoom until the rain lessened. The man didn't order anything, and I ordered Chinese quince tea. My previously explosive sentiment was automatically and ridiculously deflated after a cup of tea. I felt embarrassed for having unnecessarily scolded that young man, a mere child. Looking at Minu, I wished that I could go home and call it a day without doing laundry or cooking.

Uh, do you know by any chance, ma'am?

After sitting silently for a while, the man brought up the unexpected subject of the kindergarten disaster that had occurred in the neighboring city. Although it wasn't necessarily an appropriate subject for a rainy afternoon tearoom, I'd known about that incident. Such cases of child abuse, violence toward children, and the death of innocent children were common; but that particular incident five years ago stood apart from other child abuse cases in its size and intentionality. Three kindergarten teachers who belonged to the same friendship group set fire to their respective workplaces one after another. Forty-two children younger than five and eight kindergarten teachers had died.

Although the perpetrators were all arrested, it

인 부모라면 해서는 안 되는 일로 여겨졌다. 민우가 내 손에 맡겨진 것도 따지고 거슬러 올라가보면 그 사건 때문이었다.

남자는 천천히 말했다. 그 세 명이 일을 하며 겪어왔을지 모르는 열악한 상황과 피로가 끔찍한 범죄의 동기를 정당화해 줄 수는 없었다고. 그러나 그 사건 이후 국가적 차원에서 대책위원회가 꾸려졌고, 아이의 안전과 양육자의 복지 사이의 관계에 대해 사람들 모두가 조금 더 심각하게 생각하게 되었다고.

그런가 하며 그저 듣고 있는데 그가 말했다.

그래서 제가 태어나게 됐어요. 이렇게 얘기하면 좀 이상하지만, 저는 그 참사에서 비롯된 셈이죠.

나는 이해할 수가 없었다.

음, 아이가 아무리 힘들게 해도 저는 고통스럽지 않아요. 화가 나지도, 짜증을 느끼지도, 지치지도, 침울해지지도 않죠. 그렇게 만들어지지 않았으니까요. 그러니까, 안심하세요. 나쁜 짓은 하지 않아요.

남자가 미소 지었다.

장맛비 때문에 외출이 뜸해지자 갑갑증이 난 민우는

took awhile for the shock to subside. Also, a considerable number of daycare centers nationwide had to close their doors. People viewed leaving their babies to the hands of strangers other than family members as taboo for normal parents. It's no exaggeration to say that it was because of that incident that Minu's care fell into my hands.

He spoke slowly. The poor working condition and fatigue that the three kindergarten teachers might have experienced during their work couldn't have justified their horrific crimes. Still, after that incident, the government formed a committee to solve that problem and people began to think more seriously about the relationship between child safety and caretakers' wellbeing.

I was just listening, thinking what he said seemed to make sense, when he said,

That's why I was born. Strange to say, but I originated from that disaster.

I didn't understand.

No matter how bothersome a child is, I don't feel any pain. I don't get angry, irritated, tired, or depressed. I am not programed that way. So, don't worry. I don't do anything bad. The man smiled.

아침부터 저녁까지 내 다리에 바싹 들러붙어 치대고 보챘다. 평소의 두 배로 떼를 쓰는 아이를 달래며 나는 그에 대해 생각했다.

대니. 그게 그의 이름이었다. 미국에서 최초로 만들어졌고, 우리 상황에 맞게 약간의 개조를 거친 뒤 전국 50개 가정에 시범적으로 파견되었다고 뉴스에는 나와 있었다. 나는 그 순간 각자 어딘가에서 아기를 안은 채 기저귀 찬 엉덩이를 토닥이거나, 자장가를 부르거나, 장난감을 흔들며 놀아주고 있는 50명의 대니, 똑같은 얼굴을 한 대니들을 상상해보았다. 어쩐지 이 세상의 것같지 않은 풍경이었다.

떼쓰는 건 타고난 기질일 수도 있지만 다른 이유 때문일 수도 있어요. 사람은 누구나 마음속에 불안정한 부분이 조금씩 있는데 아이들은 자기를 돌보는 사람에게서 그걸 놀랍도록 예민하게 감지해요. 아기 이름이 민우라고 했나요?

아기 의자에 앉은 민우는 테이블 위의 냅킨을 찢으면서 놀고 있었다. 슬슬 짜증을 낼 타이밍이었는데 아니나 다를까, 더 이상 찢을 부분이 없어지자 입이 샐쭉 나오더니 힝힝 울음을 흘리기 시작했다. 그러고는 내가

As we couldn't go out often because of the rainy season, Minu stuck to my legs and threw tantrums from the morning until evening. As I tried to appease Minu, as he made twice as much trouble as before, I thought of the man.

Danny. That was his name. According to a news article, he was first made in the U.S. and distributed among 50 Korean families for a trial run after being modified a bit to fit the Korean culture. At that moment I pictured 50 Danny's with the same faces, patting diapered babies cradled in their arms, singing lullabies, or playing with babies with a gently shaking toy. The scene seemed otherworldly.

There could be reasons other than the child's inherent nature for their tantrum, ma'am. Everyone has some insecurity in his or her heart, and babies perceive it with surprising sensitivity. Was his name Minu?

Minu was sitting in his booster seat, playing with a paper napkin, tearing it to pieces. When I thought it was about time for him to begin to grow annoyed on realizing that there were no more napkins to tear, he indeed began to cry, his lips quivering and pouted. He slapped at my hand, pounded the table, and began to wail. All eyes in

내민 손을 탁 때리고, 테이블을 쾅쾅 치더니 제풀에 얼굴이 새빨개져서는 본격적으로 울어젖히는 것이었다. 찻집 안 사람들의 시선이 일제히 우리에게로 쏠렸다. 땀이 났다. 아이를 데리고 나가려고 나는 일어섰다.

제가 잠깐 안아봐도 될까요?

대니가 나를 보았다.

모과차 다 드실 동안만요.

민우가 울면 딸이 어려서 울던 게 생각났다. 평생 반쪽 사랑밖에 주지 못해 딸은 무얼 해도 아픈 손가락이었다. 나는 마지못해 자리에 앉았다. 댁이 기계라는 건 그렇다 치자. 어떻게 기계가 아이 돌보는 일을 할 수 있나. 아이는 애정을 필요로 하고, 그 애정은 아무리 서툴고 부족하다 해도 인간의 우물에서밖에 길어 올릴 수 없는 자원이 아닌가. 내 마음속의 그런 의구심이 나를 코웃음 치게 했고, 그래, 어디 한번 해봐라 하는 마음을 불렀던 것이다.

대니가 품에 안자 아이는 잠깐 당황하는 것처럼 보였다.

그리고 4, 5초쯤 지났을까. 웃는다. 민우가 방싯방싯 웃음을 짓고 있었다. 낯선 사람의 가슴에 머리를 기대고, 더없이 편안한 표정으로 웃고 있었다.

the tearoom were on us. I began to sweat. I stood up to take the baby outside.

May I hold him for a moment, ma'am?

Danny looked at me.

I'll hold him until you finish your tea, ma'am.

Whenever Minu cried, I remembered my own daughter's cries. As my daughter received only half of her parents' love, she was, to me, always like my painful finger. I sat down reluctantly. So you're a machine, that's fine. But how could a machine take care of a baby? A baby needs love, and isn't love a resource that we cannot get anywhere else but than from a human being? Doubtful thoughts like these made me sneer inside and allowed me to challenge him with Minu, as if to say to him: Okay, then, why don't you give it a try.

When Danny picked up Minu, the baby seemed a little perplexed.

Then four or five seconds later, Minu smiled. He smiled brilliantly. He leaned his head against the stranger's chest. His smile was extremely comfortable.

Look! He doesn't feel insecure, right? I don't feel any emotional insecurity, Danny said. I can help you when it's too hard for you.

보세요. 불안해하지 않죠? 저에게는 감정적 불안정이 없거든요.

대니가 말했다.

너무 힘드실 때는 제가 도와드릴 수 있어요.

그날 아이는 대니의 품에 안긴 채 잠들었다. 집에 돌아와 눕힐 때까지 깨지 않았고, 다음 날 아침까지 달게 통잠을 잤다.

종일 빗소리가 그치지 않았다. 따뜻한 물에 머리를 감고 심호흡을 오래 하고 싶었다. 입지 않던 옷을 옷장에서 꺼내 입고 싶어졌다. 나는 망설이다 전화기를 집어 들었다.

샴촌! 대니 삼촌! 나 돈!

아이가 뛰어와 조막만 한 손바닥을 벌렸다. 대니가 지갑에서 동전을 꺼내주자 아이는 그걸 대니의 얼굴로 가져갔다. 입에 밀어넣으려는 거였다.

노래해.

지희야, 삼촌한테는 돈, 넣지 않아도 돼.

대니가 웃으며 말했다.

그래도, 그래도! 정당한 대가를 지불하려고 그러는데

That day, Minu fell asleep in Danny's arms. He didn't wake up while he carried him home and laid him down. And he continued to sleep soundly until the next morning.

The sound of rain hadn't stopped all day. I wanted to wash my hair in warm water and take a deep breath. I felt like taking out and putting on clothes I hadn't worn for a long time. I hesitated a little and then picked up the phone.

Yuncle! Yuncle Danny! Me, money!

A child ran to him and opened her tiny palm. When Danny took out a coin from his purse and gave it to her, she brought it to Danny's face. She was trying to put it into Danny's mouth.

Sing.

Jihi, you don't have to put a coin into your uncle's mouth. Danny smiled and said.

But, but! I want to pay the right price, so why not take it?

The child was persistent. Danny pretended to accept the coin into his mouth and then turned around to take it out.

Which song do you want? "Galaxy Friends Forever"?

왜 싫다고 해.

아이가 고집을 피웠다. 대니는 못 이기는 척 동전을 입에 넣었다가 고개를 돌려 빼냈다.

무슨 노래 할까? 「은하친구들 영원하라」, 할까?

싫어. 그건 지겨워. 지긋지긋해!

그럼 뭐가 좋을까?

내가 모르는 노래!

잠시 생각하던 대니가 야구 모자를 고쳐 쓰고는, 자세를 바로 하고 노래를 부르기 시작했다.

아, 목동들의 피리 소리들은 산골짝마다 울려 나오고
여름은 가고 꽃은 떨어지니 너도 가고 또 나도 가야지
저 목장에는 여름철이 오고 산골짝마다 눈이 덮여도
나 항상 오래 여기 살리라
아 목동아, 아 목동아, 내 사랑아[1]

키즈카페 안에 흩어져 놀던 아이들이 사방에서 다가와 대니를 둘러쌌다. 노래가 끝났을 때는 경이에 가득 찬 표정을 한 아이들과 그 부모들로 몇 겹의 동심원이

1) 「아 목동아」, 현제명 옮김, 원곡은 「Danny Boy」.

No, I'm tired of it. Sick and tired of it!

Then, which one?

A song I don't know!

After thinking about it for a moment, Danny fixed his baseball cap, sat up straight, and began to sing.

Oh Danny boy, the pipes, the pipes are calling
From glen to glen, and down the mountainside,
The summer's gone, and all the roses falling,
'Tis you, 'tis you must go and I must bide.

But come ye back when summer's in the meadow,
Or when the valley's hushed and white with snow,
'Tis I'll be here in sunshine or in shadow,
Oh Danny boy, oh Danny boy, I love you so![1]

All the children playing all over the kid's café came toward Danny and surrounded him. When the song ended, there were several rings of bystanders around him. They were all marveling,

1) This is the lyric of "Danny Boy," a ballad written by English songwriter Frederic Weatherly (1848-1929) and usually set to the Irish tune of the "Londonderry Air."

만들어져 있었다.

우리 로봇 샴촌이야. 너흰 이런 거 없지? 짝짝짝, 박수!

선망과 질투가 뒤섞인 표정으로 아이들이 박수를 쳤다. 민우가 두 손을 맞잡고 흔들며 흥에 겨워 까르르 웃어댔다.

또 해줘.

아이들은 자리를 떠나지 않았다. 결국 대니는 다섯 곡을 더 부르고 마지막에는 자리에서 일어나 엉덩이춤까지 추었다. 나는 마술쇼를 구경하는 기분으로 얼이 빠져 앉아 있었다. 그는 조금도 지치지 않았다.

동요도 아닌데 좋아하네.

아이마다 원하는 게 달라요. 아까는 그런 분위기였어요.

그걸 알 수 있어?

저에게는 냄새를 맡거나 소리를 듣는 것과 마찬가지예요. 기저귀 가져오셨어요?

응, 왜?

1분 뒤에 민우가 응가를 할 거거든요. 제가 갈아드릴까요?

대니가 권유했지만 나는 그의 손에 민우를 맡기지는

those children and parents.

He is my robot yuncle. You don't have anything like this, right? Clap, clap!

The children clapped, their faces full of envy and jealousy. With his hands together, Minu kept giggling.

Sing again! The children didn't budge.

In the end, Danny sang five more songs and even stood up and danced during the last one. I was dazed, as if I was watching a magic show. He didn't get tired at all.

You didn't sing children's songs, but they liked them.

Children want changes all the time. The atmosphere called for those sorts of songs.

You can tell that?

To me, that's like smelling or hearing. Did you bring a diaper?

Yes, why?

Minu will need to go to the bathroom in one minute. Shall I change it for you?

Although Danny volunteered, I didn't leave Minu with him. Without Minu around I could have soaked my body for a few hours in a tub, visited an herbal

않았다. 아이 없이 두어 시간쯤 목욕물에 몸을 담그고 땀을 빼거나, 한의원에 가 새로 약을 지어오거나, 안 나간 지 십수 년인 대학 동창 모임에 나가볼 수도 있었지만 그러지 않았다. 사는 게 힘들다고 툭하면 눈물 바람인 딸아이에게 행여나 책잡힐 거리를 만들고 싶지 않기도 했지만, 결국 나는 기계를 믿을 만큼 개방적인 인간은 아니었던 것이다.

그럼에도 나는 그와 자주 만났다. 대니가 지희와 장 보는 데 따라가기도 하고, 아이들을 위한 공연을 보러 가기도, 장마 사이사이 땡볕이 내리쬐는 날엔 분수대가 있는 옆 동네 공원으로 물놀이하는 사람들 구경을 나가기도 했다. 민우를 안은 채, 반쯤은 대니가 화수분처럼 흩뜨리는 행복의 기운을 보면서도 믿지 못하는 심정으로, 또 반쯤은 바운서나 흔들 침대 같은 편리한 도구를 싼값에 얻은 아기 엄마처럼 적나라하게 고마워하는 심정을 품고.

대니에게 안겨 있으면 민우는 울지 않았다. 아이 울음소리가 없는 그 짤막한 시간들은 아찔하게 달콤하고 두려웠다. 내가 평생 삶이란 것의 본질이라 믿어온 악다구니와 발버둥이 그 시간들에서는 도려낸 것처럼 빠져

clinic to get new batches of herbal medicine, or at-
tended a college alum gathering that I hadn't been
going to for decades. But I didn't. I didn't want to
create any excuses for my daughter to blame me.
She was prone to crying, to going on about how
hard her life was. More importantly, I wasn't open-
minded enough to trust a machine.

Nevertheless, he and I met often. I followed
Danny and Jihi with Minu when they went shopping, or when we went to performances for children or to the water fountain at the park in the
neighboring town on occasional sunny days during
the rainy season. With Minu in my arms, I sat back
and watched in disbelief as Danny seemed to
spread happiness around him like an inexhaustible
treasure chest. I was also frankly half grateful for
his presence. I felt like a new mother buying
bouncers or rocking beds at bargain prices.

In Danny's arms, Minu didn't cry. Those short
moments when no child's cry could be heard were
dizzyingly sweet and terrifying. During those times
it didn't seem like our lives lacked what I had believed to be its essence, its brawls and struggles. It
felt as if they had been completely cut out of our
lives. Nobody criticized or punished me, even

있었다. 이를 악물고 두통약을 삼키지 않아도 아무도 나를 몰아세우거나 벌을 내리지 않았다. 나는 다시 밥을 천천히 씹어서 먹을 수 있게 됐고, 아이가 저지레를 쳐도 예전처럼 한숨만 한번 쉬고 안아줄 수도 있었다.

달라진 게 또 있었다. 나는 젊은 시절부터 사람을 잘 사귀는 성격이 못 됐고, 나이 들며 더 심해졌다. 3년 전 이사 온 뒤로도 동네 친구 하나 만들지 못했고, 주인과 안면을 튼 가게가 몇 집 있긴 했지만 속내를 털어놓을 정도는 아니었다. 하고 싶은 말이 있으면 모았다가 매주 화, 목, 일요일에 음식물쓰레기와 함께 배출했다. 늙으면서 자꾸만 속에 고이는 탁한 성정을 누구와 공유하는 것이 나는 내키지 않았다.

그런 내가 대니와는 실없는 말들을 제법 주고받고 있었다.

이를테면 이런 말들.

당신, 당신 하지 말고 그냥 할머니, 하면 안 되나. 듣는 입장에선 삿대질 당하는 거 같고 영 이상한데.

그런가요. 전에 어떤 분한테 실수한 적이 있어서 조심하고 있는 건데.

though I wasn't grinding my teeth or swallowing any painkillers. I could eat rice, leisurely chew it again, and I could simply pick up and hug Minu after a single sigh, even when he made a mess of the room.

There was another change, too. I hadn't been very social by nature since I was young, and this tendency had become even stronger as I grew older. Although I had moved three years before, I hadn't made a single friend in this neighborhood. I had become friendly with a few storeowners, but they weren't my friends. I simply collected all my thoughts and threw them out every Tuesday, Thursday, and Sunday together with the garbage. I didn't feel like sharing the turbid thoughts and feelings gathering inside me as I grew older.

Then, I found myself talking about meaningless things with Danny.

For example...

Don't call me just ma'am, but Grandma. Wouldn't that be better? It feels weird for someone to call me ma'am like that. It somehow feels as if I were being accused of something.

Is that so? I'm just trying to be careful, because I made a mistake before when I addressed another

무슨 실수?

할머니라고 불렀는데, 그분이 자기는 할머니 아니라고 그러시는 거예요. 그래서 죄송합니다, 아주머니, 그랬는데 아주머니도 아니라고 하셔서. 그래서, 차라리 당신이 낫지 않을까 했는데.

나는 할머니 맞으니까 괜찮아.

네, 할머니.

…….

…….

왜?

그렇게 웃으시는 건 처음인데요.

그런가.

할머니는 놀라시지 않네요.

뭐에?

제가 저에 대해 말하면 곧바로 도망치는 사람들도 많은데, 할머니는 별로 동요하시지 않아서 의외였어요.

놀라기야 놀랐지.

그래요?

사실 지금도 놀라. 같이 잘 다니다가도 아참, 사람이 아니지, 아참, 숨을 안 쉬지, 그런 생각이 퍼뜩 들 때도

older lady.

What was the mistake?

I called her Grandma, but she told me that she was *not* a grandmother. So, I said, I'm sorry, auntie. Then, she said that she wasn't an auntie, either. So, I thought, calling someone just ma'am might be better.

I'm a grandma, so you can call me Grandma.

Yes, Grandma.

I smiled and he stayed silent.

Why?

This is your first time smiling, Grandma.

Really?

You weren't surprised, by the way.

At what?

When I talk about myself, most people just run away. You weren't disturbed, so I was surprised.

I was surprised, too.

Yes?

In fact, I'm still surprised. While walking with you leisurely, I suddenly remember: right, you're not a human being. Right, you don't breathe. But since I've lived through all kinds of misfortunes and adversities, I don't get surprised that easily. That's why.

What kinds of misfortunes and adversities,

있는데 뭐. 근데 나는 그래. 평생 이런 일 저런 일 다 겪고 살다 보니 웬만한 일에는 잘 놀라지 않게 돼버렸어. 그래서 그래.

어떤 이런 일 저런 일요?

그런 게 있어.

나는 조금 웃었다. 친한 친구가 고작 서른 살에 암으로 죽어버렸어. 자고 일어났는데 살림살이에 차압 딱지가 죄 붙어 있기도 했고, 연락이 두절된 남편을 겨우 찾고 보니 다른 집에서 다른 사람들과 살고 있기도 했지. 그런 빤하고 낡아빠진 얘기들이 순식간에 목에 차오르는 게 싫어서 입을 다물었다. 기계로 된 뇌와 심장과 혀를 지닌 예쁘장한 청년이 웃으며 내 얘기를 들어주고 오후를 함께 보내주는 이런 세상이 별천지인 건 사실이었다. 잠결인지 꿈결인지 알 수 없었지만 나는 살고 있었다. 그러나 나는 어떻게 해도 대니가 온 세상, 올드타운 밖의 세상에 속할 수는 없었다.

음, 할머니?

왜?

고마워요, 놀라지 않아주셔서.

좀더 놀랄 걸 그랬나 봐.

Grandma?

This and that.

I smiled.

A close friend of mine had died of cancer when she was only thirty. Also one morning, I woke up to find our household goods had been seized. When I managed to find my runaway husband, he was living with another family in another house. Because I hated such hackneyed stories of woe and pity, which instantly filled my throat, I kept my mouth shut. This world, where a pretty young man with mechanical brain, heart, and tongue listened to me and smiled, spending afternoons with me, was indeed a brave new world. I was living in it, half sleeping and half dreaming. Nevertheless, I couldn't belong to the world that Danny came from, a world outside of this old town. It didn't matter how hard I tried.

Mmm, Grandma?

Yes?

Thank you, for not being surprised.

I should have been a little more surprised, I guess.

Wait a minute.

Danny came back with hot cocoa from a machine

잠깐만요.

대니가 조금 떨어진 자판기에서 뜨거운 코코아 한 잔을 뽑아가지고 왔다.

지희랑 민우 일어나면 달라고 난리일 테니 얼른 드세요.

나는 딱 입을 벌리고 그를 바라보았다.

왜요?

이 더운 데 이런 게 마시고 싶다니 얄궂다고 생각하고 있었는데.

음, 맞아요?

어떻게 알았어?

다행이네요.

대니가 미소지었다.

＊

질문: 아이 돌보는 일을 하기 위해 올드타운에 왔죠?
그 일이 적성에 맞았나요?

대니: 네.

질문: 아이들을 보면 어떤 생각이 드나요?

대니: 예뻐요. 사랑스럽고. 어렵기도 하고요.

a short distance away.

Drink it now, before Jihi and Minu wake up and pester you for a sip.

I stared at him, my mouth agape.

What's the matter?

I was just thinking that I had a strange craving for it in this hot weather.

Mmm, so, I was right, then?

How did you know?

I'm glad.

Danny smiled.

*

Q: You came to the old town to work as a baby-sitter, right? Did your work suit you?

Danny: Yes.

Q: When you look at children, what do you think?

Danny: They are cute. Lovely. It's hard for me as well.

Q: Hard?

Danny: Yes. I can see their desires. When I run into children in the street, I can tell that they want to eat something sweet, or they want to go some-

질문: 어려워요?

대니: 네. 아이들의 욕구가 보이니까요. 길에서 마주치는 아이들도, 달콤한 걸 먹고 싶다든지, 어디 가고 싶다든지 그런 게 몸짓이나 표정에 하나하나 드러나요. 안아줄 때 팔을 어떻게 해줬으면 좋겠다, 내가 지금 못되게 굴긴 하지만 그냥 무시해줬으면 좋겠다, 이런 것도 있어요. 아주 구체적이고 명확하죠. 그런데 그걸 제 마음대로 다 채워줄 수 없잖아요. 저는 그 아이들의 부모가 아니니까요. 그래서 행복하게 해주고 싶지만 참아요. 행동하지 않죠.

질문: 그러면, 어려워요?

대니: 네.

질문: 그럼 사진 속 이 사람을 보면 어때요?

대니: …….

질문: 아는 분인가요?

대니: 네.

질문: 이분을 처음 봤을 때 기억나요?

대니: 네. 손자를 데리고 놀이터에 계셨어요.

질문: 그때 어떤 생각을 했죠?

대니: …….

where, just by looking at their gestures or expressions. I can also tell how they want to be held by which angle of the arm, or how they want to be ignored even when they throw tantrums. Their desires are very clear, and concrete. But I cannot meet all of their desires as much as I want, right? I am not their parent. So, although I want to make them happy, I refrain from doing it. I don't always act upon it.

Q: Then, it's hard?

Danny: Yes.

Q: Then, what do you feel about this person in the photo?

Danny: (silent)

Q: You know her?

Danny: Yes.

Q: Do you remember when you first saw her?

Danny: Yes. She was with her grandson in the playground.

Q: What did you think then?

Danny: (silent)

Q: Did you tell her that she was beautiful?

Danny: ...yes.

Q: Why?

Danny: Because she was beautiful.

질문: 이분에게 아름답다고 말했나요?

대니: ……네.

질문: 왜 그랬죠?

대니: 아름다웠으니까요.

질문: 어떤 점에서요?

대니: …….

질문: 대답하기 어렵나요?

대니: ……네.

질문: 그건 당신 자신의 생각인가요?

대니: 저, 부탁이 있는데요. 잠깐 쉬었다가 하면 안 될까요?

*

누룽지탕을 먹는데 잘 먹을 수가 없었다. 가슴이 두근거려 약을 한 알 삼켰다. 그때까지만 해도 별 생각이 없었다. 늙으면 누구나 아기로 변해간다는 생각, 남에게 내 기저귀를 보여서는 안 되니 조심해야 한다는 생각이 들었을 뿐이다.

나는 무방비 상태였다. 아침에 일어나면서부터 아이

Q: In what way?

Danny: (silent)

Q: Do you find it hard to answer that question?

Danny: ...yes.

Q: Was that thought your own?

Danny: Excuse me, may I ask you a favor? Can we take a break?

*

I was eating *nurungjitang*, but I couldn't swallow it very well. As my heart began to pound, I took a pill. I didn't think much of it then. I just thought that everyone becomes a baby when they are old and that I should be careful because I didn't want to show my diaper to others.

I was helpless. The moment I got up every morning, I was attacked by the smell of the baby's excrement and of milk. What more could I have? In this dull and noble labor that continued every day without exception amidst the sound of the baby's gurgling, the sight of cooked grains of rice dotted here and there, the smell of chopped potatoes and carrots, urine, sweat, and eczema cream? What else would I be other than a crumbling, flimsy shell of a

의 똥냄새, 우유 냄새로 둘러싸여 있었다. 설마 무엇이
더 있을까. 옹알거리는 소리, 사방에 묻은 밥풀이며 잘
게 자른 감자와 당근 쪼가리, 오줌과 땀과 습진 크림, 그
사이로 하루도 거르지 않고 이어지는 이 둔하고 숭고한
노동 속에. 매일 삶는 거즈손수건처럼 하얗게 바짝 말
라 귀퉁이마다 파삭거리는 존재 말고 내가 달리 무엇이
겠나. 나는 그렇게만 생각했다. 아이는 날마다 나가서
놀아야 했고 놀이터는 집에서 너무 가까웠다. 나는 내게
일어나고 있는 일이 뭔지 몰랐고, 알고 싶지도 않았다.

　그런 식으로 일어나는 일들도 있었다.

　여긴 왜 이래요?
　젊었을 때 프라이팬에, 뭐였지, 생선 튀기다 기름이
튀었나 그래.
　그럼 여기는요?
　애 업고 급하게 밥 차리다 압력솥 증기가 나와 데었지.
　그게 언젠데요?
　한참 전이지. 40년도 넘게 전이네.
　그런데 아직까지 이래요?
　그러게. 없어질 줄 알았는데 안 없어지네.

being, like the dried, pale gauze napkin that I boiled every day? That was all I thought about myself. Minu had to go out and play every day, and the playground was so close to my apartment. I did not know what was happening to me and I didn't want to know either.

Some things happen that way.

What happened here?

When I was young, let me see, I think that oil dropped from the frying pan while I was frying fish.

How about here?

The steam from my pressure cooker burned me when I was hurrying to set the table. I was piggy-backing my child.

When was that?

It's been a while. More than forty years ago.

It's still there, though?

I guess. I thought it would go away, but it didn't.

It looks like a map.

I think so, too.

This here is a continent, and that's an island.

That's right. You couldn't draw it if you wanted to.

Why don't you have a toenail here?

지도 같은데요.

내가 봐도 그래.

여기는 대륙이고, 여기는 섬이네요.

그러게. 일부러 이렇게 그리래도 못 그리겠어.

이 발톱은 왜 빠졌어요?

몰라. 산에 갔다 내려와서 양말을 벗어보니 그냥 빠졌어. 병원에 갔더니 그런 일이 간혹 있다고 하데.

아팠겠네요.

그때는 무지 아팠는데, 지금은 보면 그냥 웃겨. 그때 같이 간 사람들이 김밥이랑 만두를 싸 왔는데, 김밥에 든 멸치가 너무 매워서 다 같이 배탈이 났었거든. 산에 화장실이 없어서 막 뛰어서 내려왔지. 열 명이나 되는 사람들이 전부.

와.

지금 그 사람들 다 뭐하나. 둘은 죽었고, 나머지는 연락이 안 되는데.

궁금해요?

여긴 왜 이래?

네? 뭐가요?

어째 이리 상처도 흉도 하나 없어. 애 보는 사람이.

I don't know. I came down from a mountain and took off my sock to find it like that. I went to the hospital, but the doctor said that this kind of thing happened occasionally.

It must have hurt.

It hurt a lot then, but I think it's funny now. Some people brought *kimbop* and *mandu* to the mountain. The anchovy inside the *kimbop* was so spicy that we all had terrible stomach trouble. Since there was no toilet in the mountain, we all ran madly down together. All ten of us.

Wow.

What are they all doing now?

Two died, and I haven't heard from the rest.

Are you curious about them?

Why are you like this, Danny?

What do you mean, Grandma?

How come you don't have any scars at all? You, a babysitter?

That's right. Oh, I have a scar here.

What is it?

It's a galaxy friend character stamp. Because Jihi didn't want it, I took it instead, but it doesn't erase.

Good. It won't be erased. That's too bad.

It won't erase even after forty years?

그러게요. 아, 여기 하나 있다.

이게 뭐야?

은하친구들 캐릭터 도장요. 지희가 안 받는다고 해서 제가 대신 받았는데 안 지워져요.

잘했다. 안 지워질 거야. 너 이제 큰일 났다.

40년 지나도 안 지워질까요?

40년 지나도 안 지워져.

그러면 좋겠다.

왜?

할머니랑 이 얘기한 거 기억날 테니까요.

좋아하는 것들을 하나씩 말하는 게임도 했었다.

내가 좋아하는 것들은, 주인 없는 집 담장 안에 소담스럽게 핀 능소화(능소화가 뭐죠? 잠깐만요, 이제 알겠어요). 꽃집 진열대에 걸린 채 사람들의 호기심 어린 시선을 견디는 벌레잡이통풀의 벌레주머니(왜 호기심 어린 시선이에요? 왜 견디죠?). 집 나간 고양이를 걱정하는 옆 건물 노파의 울음소리(어떻게 생긴 고양이였어요?). 그 소리를 듣고 무슨 일이냐고 묻는 사람들의 목소리(찾았나요?). 잠든 아이의 이마에 살짝 배어난 땀냄새(그건 나도 좋아해

It won't.

I'd like that.

Why?

I'll remember our talk today.

We also played a game where we talked about things we liked.

I liked a nice, delicious-looking trumpet creeper on the walls of an empty house (What is a trumpet creeper? Wait. Oh, I get it now.). The monkey cups that hang from the display case in the flower shop and must endure people's curious, lingering stares (Why curious? Why lingering?). The sound of the old woman crying in the adjacent building when she worries about her runaway cat (How did the cat look?). The sound of people asking her why she cried after they heard her cry (Did she find the cat?). The smell of a thin layer of sweat on a sleeping baby's forehead (I like it, too.). The long fingers of a good-natured young man smiling at a baby.

What Danny liked were mostly words. They were words that I wasn't sure if he understood their meanings. For example, family, love, hope, sorrow, self-reliance, independence, reconciliation, memory, forgiveness. And then there was baby, babies,

요). 그런 아이를 보고 웃는 마음 착한 청년의 긴 손가락.

대니가 좋아하는 것들은 주로 단어들이었다. 그가 의미를 알고 있는지 아닌지 모를 단어들. 이를테면 가족, 사랑, 희망, 슬픔, 자립, 독립, 화해, 추억, 용서. 그리고 아이, 아이들, 엉덩이, 뽀뽀, 잼잼, 곤지곤지, 도리도리, 응가, 쉬, 엄마, 아빠, 할머니, 24(저는 태어났을 때 스물네 살이었고 앞으로도 스물네 살이겠죠. 스물네 살에 할머니는 뭘 했어요?).

엄마, 듣고 있어? 다음 주에는 우리, 못 올 것 같다고요.

왜?

일주일 휴간데, 은영이라고 내 친구 있잖아? 걔네 부부랑 같이 태국 여행 다녀오려고. 엄마도 알잖아, 우리 결혼하고 3년 동안 아무데도 못 간 거. 미안해요. 민우는 다다음 주에 데리러 올게. 그래도 되지?

나는 그러라고, 조심해서 다녀오라고 말하려고 했다. 그런데 입에서 다른 말이 튀어나와버린 모양이었다. 딸아이가 당황한 얼굴로 나를 보며 물었다.

엄마, 지금 뭐라고 그랬어?

응?

같이…… 가면 좋겠다고 그러지 않았어?

butt, kiss, close-them-open-them, point-here-point-there, turn-it-turn-it, poop, pee, mommy, daddy, grandma, twenty-four (I was born twenty-four years old and I'll always be twenty-four. What did you do when you were twenty-four, Grandma?)

Mom, are you listening? We cannot come next week.

Why?

We have a week's vacation. You remember Eun-yeong, my friend? We're going to Thailand with Eunyeong and her husband. You understand, Mom, right? We haven't been anywhere for three years since we married. I'm sorry. We'll get Minu the week after. That's okay with you, right?

I meant to say, Please do, please have a nice trip. But it seems that something else leapt out of my mouth. My daughter turned around to look at me, her face suddenly flushed.

Mom, what did you just say?

Mmm?

Did, did you say: that you'd like to go with us?

Did I?

Why didn't you tell me before? I'm even more sorry to hear it from you. You've never said any-

내가?

그럼 미리 말을 하지. 생전 그런 말 안 하던 사람이 그러니까 더 미안하네.

내가 그랬나.

같이는…… 못 갈 것 같은데. 민우는 아직 너무 어리고, 엄마도 몸이 안 좋잖아.

그래.

서운해?

아니야, 서운하긴. 잘 다녀와.

다음에는 꼭 같이 가자.

그래!

가벼운 마른기침을 하던 민우가 열이 오르면서 기침이 심해지고 분수토를 하기 시작한 건 딸아이 부부가 출국한 다음 날이었다. 해열제를 먹이고 얼음 수건 찜질을 해도 열이 40도에서 내려가지 않아 큰 병원까지 가야 했다. 급성폐렴에 인두염이 겹쳤으니 바로 입원하라는 소견이 나왔다. 두꺼운 링거 바늘을 꽂고 침대에 눕히자 아이는 아픈 것보다 답답한 게 싫은지 일어났다 앉았다 하며 병실이 떠나가도록 기침 반 눈물 반 울어

thing like that before.

Haven't I?

I don't... I don't think we can take you. Minu's too young, and you're not very well.

Okay.

Are you upset?

No, why would I be upset? Have a nice trip.

We'll go together next time, I promise.

Okay!

It was the day after my daughter and her husband left for Thailand when Minu, who had been coughing light, dry coughs, developed a fever, severe coughing, and severe vomiting. I gave him medicine for the fever and applied ice towels but his fever stayed at 40 degrees Celsius. I had to take him to a large hospital. I was told to have him hospitalized immediately because he had acute pneumonia and pharyngitis. As he lay on the bed with a thick needle sticking out of him for an administration of Ringer's solution, Minu wailed and hacked sharply. Perhaps more than being sick he didn't like being restrained.

The moment Minu just fell asleep and I finally had time to breathe, I called my daughter. My daughter's

됐다.

아이가 겨우 잠들어 자리 비울 틈이 났을 때 딸아이에게 전화를 걸었다. 잠에서 덜 깬 목소리로 전화를 받은 딸은 바로 울먹이기 시작했다. 그러니까 내가 애 데리고 너무 나다니지 말라고 그랬잖아! 윙윙거리는 소음 속에서 딸이 뭐라고 소리를 질렀고 전화가 끊어졌다. 나는 홀로그램 전화가 걸려오거나 딸아이가 바로 돌아올 줄 알고 기다렸다.

지금도 가끔 생각한다. 그때 딸아이가 바로 돌아왔더라면, 혹은 하루만 일렀더라면 무언가가 달라졌을까. 다 부질없는 생각들이다.

함께 있던 환자가 항의를 해서 둘째 날에 아이를 1인실로 옮겼다. 간신히 열이 조금 내리자 이번에는 가래가 너무 심해졌다. 아이는 잠을 못 자고 밤새 콜록거리며 보챘고, 사흘이 지나도록 상태는 나아지지 않았다. 나는 지하에 있는 편의점에서 속옷을 사 입고 화장실에서 머리를 감았다. 나흘째 되던 날, 보다 못한 간호사가 와서 말했다. 제가 아이 잠깐 봐드릴 테니 옆방에서 한 시간만 편히 주무세요.

옆방은 6인실이었고, 침대 하나가 비어 있었다. 올라

voice was thick with sleep but she began to cry immediately. Didn't I tell you not to take him outdoors so often? She kept on yelling amidst humming noises and then the phone disconnected. Thinking that she would either call me through the hologram phone or she would return home right away, I waited.

I still occasionally wonder. If only she returned right away then, or, if only Minu had gotten sick a day earlier, then would the results have been different? These are all useless thoughts now though.

Because the patient in the other room protested, Minu was moved to a single room the next day. His fever barely lowered, but then he began to suffer from severe phlegm build-up. Minu couldn't sleep and simply coughed through the night. His symptoms didn't improve after three days. I bought underwear from the convenience store at the basement of the hospital and washed my hair in the bathroom. On the fourth day, a sweet nurse came in and said, I'll take care of the baby for a while. Why don't you have a nap for an hour in the room next door?

The room next door was a six-bed room and there was one empty bed. I clambered into the bed

가 누우니 신음이 나올 만큼 편했다. 꼭 한 시간이라고 생각하며 눈을 감고 있는데, 전화기에 메시지가 수신되었다.

생일 축하해요, 할머니.
-DANNY

일찍 오지 못해서 미안해요. 이번 주부터는 지희 영재 스쿨 시간표가 바뀌어서 어쩔 수 없었어요.

와달라고 연락한 거 아닌데 왜 왔어. 이 시간에 나오면 지희 엄마 아빠가 이상하게 생각하지 않아?

음, 한 달에 한두 번은 괜찮아요. 그렇게 정해져 있어요.

지희가 자다 깰 수도 있는데.

할머니, 아프죠?

응?

무릎이 아픈가요? 잠을 못 잤어요?

이 나이에 여기저기 아픈 거야 지극히 정상이고, 어제는 그제보다 많이 잤어. 그제는 그그저께보다 많이 잤고.

잠을 자지 못하면 힘들죠?

좋지야 않지.

and lay down. It was so comfortable I almost moaned aloud. I closed my eyes, thinking that I'd sleep just for an hour, when I received a message on my phone:

Happy Birthday, Grandma.
- Danny

I'm sorry that I didn't come earlier. I couldn't help it because the schedule at the School for the Gifted that Jihi attends changed this week.

I didn't let you know to ask you to come. Why did you come? Wouldn't Jihi's mom and dad be concerned if you left home at this hour?

Um, it's okay once or twice a month. That's how it's supposed to be.

Jihi might wake up.

Grandma, you don't look well.

Really?

Do you have pain in your knees? Haven't you had enough sleep?

It's extremely normal for me at my age to have aches here and there. I slept more last night than the night before. And more this night than the night before.

음.

잠을 자지 않으니까 모르겠네, 참.

미안해요. 몰라서. 잠을 자지 않아서, 몰라서.

…….

왜 웃어요?

아냐. 민우가 한결 표정이 낫네. 웃다가 금방 잠드는 게 신기해. 목이 부어서 아직도 밥을 못 넘기고 흰죽만 겨우 먹는 놈이.

당연하죠, 제가 왔는데.

어떻게 하지.

뭘요?

아냐.

이거 드세요. 할머니 좋아하시는 양갱 사 왔어요. 저녁은 드셨어요?

…….

할머니.

응.

왜 그래요? 또 안 먹는다. 누구 좋아하면 먹을 게 안 넘어간다면서, 할머니는 내가 그렇게 좋아요?

대니.

It's hard if you don't have enough sleep, isn't it?

It's not comfortable.

Umm...

You wouldn't know because you don't sleep, huh!

I'm sorry I don't know. Because I don't sleep and because I don't know.

I didn't respond.

Why are you laughing, Grandma?

I'm not. Minu looks much better. It's strange that he was laughing and then he just fell asleep right away. His throat is so swollen he still can't eat rice and eats only rice porridge.

It's natural for him to fall asleep, because I'm here.

What should I do?

What are you talking about?

Nothing.

Here, take this. I brought the sweet jelly of beans that you like. Have you had dinner?

I didn't respond.

Grandma.

Yes.

What's wrong? You're not eating again. You said you couldn't swallow food if you liked somebody. Do you like me so much, Grandma?

네.

와줘서 고마워. 양갱 사다준 것도 고맙고, 생일 축하해준 것도, 미안하다고 해준 것도 고마워. 그런데 이제 오지 마. 앞으로는 우리 연락하지 말고 보지도 말자.

네? 그게 무슨 말이에요?

무슨 말이냐면, 앞으로는 너와 연락하고 싶지도 보고 싶지도 않다는 말이야. 네가 잘해줄수록 나는 괴로워. 알겠지?

*

질문: 다시 말할 수 있겠어요?

대니: 네.

질문: 친구라고 했나요?

대니: 네. 할머니를 멀리서 처음 봤을 때, 친구를 만난 거라고 생각했어요. 그러니까, 또 다른 나요. 또 다른 대니.

질문: 무슨 뜻이죠?

대니: 저와 같은 사람인 줄 알았어요. 표정도 그랬고, 몸을 움직이는 모습도요. 쉬지 않았어요. 저처럼요. 아기를 돌보고, 행복하게 해주고 싶어 하는 사람이었어

Danny?

Yes?

Thank you for coming. Thank you for the bring-
ing sweet jelly of beans, for celebrating my birthday, for saying sorry. But don't come and see me
anymore. Let's not contact or see each other from
now on.

What? What are you talking about?

I'm saying that I don't want to contact or see you
anymore. The kinder you act the more painful it is
for me. Got it?

*

Q: Can you tell me again?

Danny: Yes.

Q: Did you say, "friend?"

Danny: Yes. When I first saw Grandma, I thought
I had met a friend. That is, another me, another
Danny.

Q: What do you mean?

Danny: I thought she was like me. Her facial expression, and the way she moved. She never took
a rest. Like me. She was someone who wanted to
take care of and make the baby happy. I heard that

요. 다른 AB들이 어딘가 있다고 들었는데, 올드타운에는 저 혼자라 궁금했어요. 그런데 그런 사람이 또 있는 거예요.

질문: 그래서 말을 걸고 싶었나요?

대니: 네. 그런데 가까이서 보니, 아니었어요. 땀을 흘리고 있었고, 그리고…… 저와는 달랐어요.

질문: 어떻게 달랐는지 설명할 수 있나요?

대니: 할머니는, 견디고 있었어요. 저는 견디지 않아도 되거든요.

질문: 견뎌요? 아까 아이들을 돕지 못하면 어려워진다고 했는데, 그것과 견디는 것은 다른가요?

대니: 음, 네. 저에게는 매 순간이, 말하자면 사람들이 맛있는 음식을 먹는 것과 같아요. 농구공을 골대에 넣는 것과 같죠. 나를 필요로 하는 누군가가 있고 그 사람을 행복하게 해요. 그게 저의 기쁨이에요. 그다음은 없어요. 기쁘지만, 없어요. 그래서 저는 움직여요. 만약 한 사람을 돕지 못해 어려워지면 다른 곳으로 가서 다른 사람을 도와요. 그럼 어려움은 없어져요.

질문: 아하.

대니: 그 일을 영원히 계속하죠. 오직 나를 위해서요.

there were other ABs, but I seemed like the only AB in the old town. So I wondered. Then I found her—she was just like me.

Q: So, that's why you wanted to talk to her?

Danny: Yes. But when I went near her, she was not an AB. She was sweating and... She looked different.

Q: Can you tell me how she was different from you?

Danny: Grandma was enduring. I don't have to endure.

Q: Enduring? You said a while ago that you find it hard when you don't help children. So how is it different from enduring?

Danny: Well, so, to me, every moment is like the moment a human being eats something delicious. Or like making the winning shot in a basketball game. There's someone who needs me and I make them happy. That's my happiness. There's nothing other than that. I'm happy, but there's nothing. So, I keep moving. If I find it hard because I don't need to help one person, then I go to another. Then, I don't feel any difficulties any more.

Q: Ah-ha!

Danny: I work like that forever. Only for myself...

……그런데 할머니는 그렇지 않았어요. 할머니의 어떤 어려움은 없어지지 않는 것 같았어요. 견디는 거죠, 그런 건? 같이 시간을 보내는 동안 알게 된 거예요. 다른 게 또 있어요. 할머니는 행복한 순간에도 견딜 때가 있었고, 견디는 순간에도 맛있는 음식을 먹는 것 같은 표정일 때가 있었어요. 저에게는 그게 의미가 있었어요.

질문: 아름다웠나요?

대니: 잘은 모르겠어요. 내가 그 순간 무슨 의미로 그 말을 했는지요. 몰라서 미안해요.

질문: 대니, 사과할 필요는 없어요.

대니: 네. 하지만, 할머니를 보고 있으면 할머니가 영원히 계속 그 자리에 있을 것 같았어요. 저와 얘기를 나누면서요. 저는 그게 좋았어요. 하지만 그렇게 되지는 않겠죠. 이제 제가 여기 있으니, 저도 영원하지 않겠죠.

질문: 꼭 그렇지는 않아요.

대니: 그럴 수도 있죠. 그렇지 않을 수도 있고.

질문: 그래요.

대니: 그것도 알게 됐어요. 이럴 수도 저럴 수도 있다는 것.

질문: 그게 당신에게 의미 있나요?

But, Grandma was different. Some of her difficulties didn't seem to go away. That's enduring, right? I came to understand that spending time with her. There's another thing, too. Grandma endured sometimes even when she was happy. And even when she was enduring, she had an expression like she was eating something delicious. To me, that was meaningful.

Q: That was beautiful?

Danny: I'm not sure. I don't know why I said that at that moment. I'm sorry that I don't know.

Q: Danny, you don't have to apologize.

Danny: Okay. But, when I was looking at Grandma, I felt like she would be in the same place forever. Forever talking with me. But that wouldn't be. Since I'm here now, I won't be forever, either.

Q: That's not necessarily true.

Danny: That might be. And might not be.

Q: That's right.

Danny: I came to learn that, too. That things could be this way or that way.

Q: Is that meaningful to you?

Danny: Yes, I think so.

*

대니: 네, 그런 것 같아요.

*

여름은 지나가고 아이는 자란다. 민우를 보면 시간이 얼마나 빠르게 흐르는지 알 수 있다. 딸아이가 엊그제 내게 선물을 가져왔다. 두툼한 뭉치였다. 포장을 뜯어 보니 무릎에 붙이는 통증 완화 밴드가 나왔다. 민우가 사라고 시켰다고 한다. 할머니 무릎에 붙이고 얼른 나으시라고.

그리고 무슨 말들이 더 남아 있을까. 나는 이 이야기를 올드타운 속의 날들처럼 안전하고 나른한 감상 속에서 끝낼 수도 있다. 내가 대니에게 검버섯과 버섯의 차이를 설명해준 최초이자 마지막 사람일 거라는 이야기를 하거나, 그날 밤 그가 나에게 했던 말들을 태연히 나열하면서.

그렇다. 나는 확실히 그런 이야기를 잘할 수 있다. 이를테면 이런 말들.

처음에는 잘 느껴지지 않았어요. 할머니가 무얼 원하는지, 무얼 하고 싶은지. 그런데 조금씩 잘 보이고 들리

Summer passes and children grow. When I look at Minu, I know how fast time flies. My daughter brought me a gift a couple of days ago. It was a thick package. When I opened it, there were pain-alleviating knee-patches. My daughter told me that Minu asked her to get them for me, saying that Grandma could stick them on her knees and get better quickly.

And what more is there to say? I can finish this story in that safe and languid sentiment, like days in the old town. I can say that I was the first, and perhaps the last person who explained to him the difference between mushrooms and the dark mushroom spots that the elderly have on their skin. Or I can just say again what he said that night.

Yes. Certainly I could tell a story like that very well. A story like the following, for example.

In the beginning I couldn't feel what you wanted very well, Grandma, or what you wanted to do. But, gradually, I could see and hear better. I can see now, too.

That's what he told me that day, and that was true.

So why are you telling me to go? Do you hate

게 됐어요. 지금도 보여요. 그는 내게 그렇게 말했고 이 것은 거짓이 아니다. 그런데 왜 가라고 하죠? 나를 미워 하나요? 그는 내가 울음을 그칠 때까지 내 어깨를 안아 주었고, 이것 또한 거짓이 아니다.

집이 있다면 좋겠어요. 그래서 할머니와 같이 살 수 있다면 좋을 텐데.

별 소리를 다 한다.

사람들이 집에 살려면 돈이 필요하죠?

필요하지.

얼마나 필요해요? 백만 원? 2백만 원?

나는 웃었다. 집을 사는 게 아니라 빌리는 거야. 보통 은 그래. 그리고 최소한 천만 원은 있어야 빌릴 수 있고, 다달이 방세를 내야 해. 아무리 낡은 집이라도.

그렇군요.

그래.

천만 원이 있으면 할머니하고 민우하고 지희하고, 대 니하고, 같이 있을 수 있겠네요.

그래, 그럼 네가 벌어 와.

싫어요. 할머니가 가져오세요.

싫다.

me?

He held me in his arms until I stopped crying, and that was true.

I wish I had a house. I wish I could live with you, Grandma, there.

What nonsense!

You need money to live in a house, right?

Right.

How much? A million *won*? Two million *won*?

I smiled. You rent, you don't buy a house. That's usually the case. You need at least ten thousand *won* to rent a house. You have to pay monthly rent, too. No matter how old that house is.

I see.

Yeah.

So if I have ten thousand *won*, then we could live all together, you, Minu, and Jihi, and Danny, right?

Right. So go make some money.

No, you bring it, Grandma.

I don't want to.

Grandma, let's live together.

I mimed punching him in the forehead and laughed. Then I told him once again not to contact me.

He asked me if that was what I really wanted. I

할머니, 우리 같이 살아요.

나는 그의 머리에 알밤을 먹이고 웃었다. 그러고는 연락하지 말라고 그에게 한 번 더 말했다.

진심이냐고 그는 물었다. 진심이라고 나는 대답했다. 그는 돌아갔고, 다시 연락하지 않았다.

연락이 두절되었던 딸은 비행기 자리가 나지 않아 도저히 방법이 없었다면서 엿새째 되던 날 아침 일찍 돌아왔다. 딸은 많이 울었고, 민우는 겨우 상태가 호전되어 퇴원했다. 주위를 경계하며 한 발짝 한 발짝 겨우 걸음마를 하던 아이는 호되게 앓고 나자 오히려 기운이 나는지 위태롭게나마 쿵쿵거리며 뛰어다니기 시작했다. 얼마 뒤, 나는 조사를 받기 위해 나와달라는 전화를 받았다. 이 모든 일들은 거짓이 아니다.

그러나 그 전화를 받기 전, 나도 전화를 걸었다.

나는 수도 없이 대니에게 전화를 걸었다. 짐짓 단호한 척, 명령하는 어조를 골랐던 나를 후회하면서. 그때까지 한 번도 부끄러워한 적 없는 내 늙음을 부끄러워하고, 내게는 없다고 믿었던 감정들이 덩굴손처럼 집요하게 마음을 휘감고 뻗어가는 것에 당황했으나 멈출 수

said yes. He left and never contacted me.

My daughter, who hadn't called me all the while, came in early that morning on the sixth day, saying that she hadn't been able to get a plane ticket. My daughter cried and Minu finally got better and was discharged. After carefully toddling around for a while, Minu began to run around somewhat pre-cariously, perhaps enjoying the renewed sense of power after his traumatic illness. A little while later, I received a phone call summoning me to the in-vestigation. All this is true.

But before I received a phone call, I called, too.

I called Danny again and again. Regretting that I pretended to be resolute and had ordered him gone. Feeling that I couldn't help myself, even when I felt ashamed by my old age—which I had never felt ashamed of until then—even when I felt embarrassed at myself for my feelings, which I'd believed I hadn't had. Feelings reaching out like obstinate tendrils within myself.

Danny didn't answer my calls. I kept on calling. I saw him piggybacking Jihi and smiling in the play-ground. I saw that smile absentmindedly shine like a bright light, like the time when we first met. I saw

없다고 생각하면서.

대니는 받지 않았다. 나는 계속 전화를 걸었다. 놀이
터에서 지희를 업은 채 웃고 있는 그를, 마치 처음 만났
을 때처럼 환한 빛 속에서 무심하게 부서지는 그 미소
를, 그의 곁에 있는 다른 사람들을 발견할 때까지. 그는
나를 보았고, 아무 내색도 하지 않았다.

나는 잘 모르는 사람들에게도 전화를 걸었다. 이해할
수 없어 하는 그들에게 질문을 하고, 대답을 듣고, 또 질
문을 했다. 어떤 사람들은 불쾌해했고, 또 다른 사람들
은 나를 이상하게 여겼다. 가까스로 멈추어야 한다는
생각이 들었을 때, 누군가의 입에서 지희의 부모가 의
도한 것인지도 모른다는 이야기가 나왔다. 어떤 사람들
은 사람을 먼저 의심했다. 드문 일이었다.

나는 그 흐름을 따라가볼 수도 있었다. 모든 것에서
공평한 거리를 두고 처음부터 다시 살펴보자고 할 수도
있었다. 대로변에 바위를 떨어뜨려놓은 것이 다름 아닌
나라는 사실을 늦게나마 밝힐 수도, 그 바위에게는 잘
못이 없다는 사실을 말하고, 원래 있던 곳으로 돌려놓
자고 제안할 수도 있었다. 그러나 그러지 않았다. 나는
미웠고, 두려웠다. 불편을 피하고 싶었으며, 귀찮았고,

other people near him. He saw me, and didn't seem to recognize me.

I called people I didn't know very well. I asked them questions, listened to their answers, and then questioned them again. They didn't seem to understand me. Some seemed to find me unpleasant, others found me strange. When I finally thought I'd better stop, somebody said that Jihi's parents might have intentionally done it. Some people suspected human beings before they suspected machines. It was a rarity.

I could have followed that clue. I could have proposed that we examine the matter from the beginning from a fair distance. I could have confessed that it was me who had dropped that rock in the main street and then proposed to bring it back to where it was, saying that it wasn't the rock's fault. But I didn't. I hated, and I was afraid. I wanted to avoid any inconveniences. I was annoyed. I was busy.

And then, there was that one last hour in that room. He was sitting in his faded yellow T-shirt and jeans. He didn't move at all, and he didn't smile at me.

바빴다.

　그리고 그 방에서의 마지막 한 시간이 있다. 물 빠진 노란색 티셔츠와 청바지를 입고 그는 자리에 앉아 있었다. 거의 움직이지 않았고, 나를 보고도 웃지 않았다.

　나는 할 수 있는 것을 모두 했다. 학습하지 않고도 지을 수 있는 표정과 충분한 체액이 있었으므로. 나는 웃음을 지었고, 변명했고, 외면했고, 원망했다. 아무것도 모르는 척 민우 이야기, 우리가 질리도록 나누었던 아이 키우는 이야기로 화제를 돌려보기도 했다. 하염없이 말을 이어가다 물을 마셨고, 과장된 몸짓을 해보였으며, 도리어 화를 내다 마지막에는 눈물까지 흘렸다. 그러나 다른 것을 다 했어도 그에게 미안하다는 말을 할 수는 없었다.

　대니, 스물네 살의 안드로이드 베이비시터. 그가 마지막으로 내게 건넨 말은 기억할 수가 없다. 그 방에 표정이라는 것이 모두 뽑혀 나간 얼굴로 앉아 있던 청년이 정말로 대니였는지 나는 확신할 수 없으므로.

　말들은 장식이다. 혹은 허상이다. 기억은 사람을 살게

I did everything I could. I had natural facial expressions that I didn't have to learn and I had enough bodily fluids. I smiled. I brought up excuses. I turned my face. I blamed him. Pretending that nothing had changed, I talked about Minu and childrearing, a topic we'd long talked about until we grew tired of it. I talked on and on, drank water, made larger and larger gestures, burst into anger for no reason, and then even shed tears in the end. I did everything, but I still couldn't apologize.

Danny, a 24-year-old android babysitter. I cannot remember what he last said to me. I cannot be sure if that young man sitting in that room with a face completely devoid of any expression was really Danny.

Words are mere decorations. Phantoms. Memories sustain us, but they are mostly like holograms. Danny accepted his end without saying a word. I am seventy-two, and I loved and killed him. Nobody knows that. Everything fades and disappears, but this remains an unchangeable fact. And I live on and endure it.

Translated by Jeon Seung-hee

해주지만 대부분 홀로그램에 가깝다. 대니는 아무 말도 하지 않은 채 주어진 끝을 받아들였다. 나는 일흔두 살이고, 그를 사랑했고, 죽였다. 아무도 그것을 알지 못한다. 모든 것이 희미하게 사라져가지만 그 사실은 변하지 않고, 나는 여전히 살아 그것을 견딘다.

창작노트
Writer's Note

임신과 출산, 육아를 거치면서 여성의 몸과 마음은 두 개의 극단에 동시에 존재할 것을 강요받는다. 한쪽은 신의 세계이며 다른 한쪽은 짐승의 세계이다. 한쪽에는 감히 인간의 고통 따위는 발도 들여놓지 못할 만큼 무한한 사랑과 인내가 지배하는 신전이 있다. 다른 한쪽에는 똥과 오줌, 젖과 침, 땀, 피, 눈물, 토사물과 하루 15시간 이상의 반복적이고 강도 높은 육체노동이 끊임없이 쏟아져 내리는 세계, 생각하거나 꿈꾸는 것은 물론이고 원할 때 자거나 먹거나 배설할 자유조차 허락되지 않는 한시적인 감옥이 있다. 엄마가 되어 도움 받지 않고 아이를 키우는 여성들은 인간이 아닌 채 두 세계

Throughout pregnancy, childbirth, and childrearing, the woman's body and mind are forced to exist
in two extreme spaces simultaneously. One is the
world of God and the other is the world of the ani-
mal. On one side, there is a shrine, governed by an
inexhaustible love and patience, where human pain
wouldn't dare venture. On the other side, there is
the world of excrement and urine, of milk and spit,
of blood, sweat, tears, vomit, and the repetitive and
highly intensive physical labor of more than 15
consecutive hours a day that must shower down
endlessly upon the individual body, a temporary
prison where one is not only prevented from even
thinking or dreaming, but also sleeping, eating, or

사이를 분열적으로 오가지만, 그 고통이 너무 오래되고 너무 유명한 개념이 되어버린 까닭에 아무런 관심도 받지 못한다.

그나마 엄마들은 나은 편이다. 직장에 나가야 생계가 유지되는 자식들로 인해 손자 손녀의 육아를 떠맡게 된 노인들은, 돌봄노동 자체에서 오는 소외감에 더해 또 다른 소외감에 갇힌다. 그들은 원래부터 감정이나 욕망을 지닌 인간으로 여겨진 적이 별로 없었다. 오후의 어린이놀이터 벤치를 가득 메운 그들은 마치 개수대 구멍들처럼 앉아 있다. 누군가 치르지 않으면 안 되는 고역, 오물과 찌꺼기들이 수없이 그들에게 흘러간다. 그들을 볼 수 있는 사람은 드물고, 그들이 고통스러울 거라고 짐작하는 사람은 더 드물다.

하지만 누가 이런 얘기를 읽고 싶어 할까. 이런 건 말하자면 군대 얘기, 축구 얘기, 군대에서 축구한 얘기나 마찬가지 아닐까.

그래도,

무언가를 발명해서 그들에게 선물하고 싶었다. 그들을 잠시나마 인간의 상태로 회복시켜 주는 것, 그들이

even visiting the bathroom freely. Mothers who raise their children without any help must go back and forth between these two opposing worlds, as a sort of non-human being. And yet, because these pains have been long-standing and well known, no one pays any attention to their plight.

Mothers have it a little better, though, compared to grandmothers. The elderly, who are forced to take on childrearing duties because their children can barely subsist themselves, are imprisoned in a sense of isolation, not only because of their care-taking duties but also as a result of prejudices. In many ways the elderly have never really been considered human beings with feelings and desires. They sit around on playground benches in the afternoon, like sink holes. They are the receptacles for the toil that somebody has to take on, for the soil and garbage that flow down endlessly toward them. People rarely see them, and people who can imagine their pain are even rarer.

But who would want to read a story about that? It would be like reading a story about compulsory military service period, or one's trials on the soccer field, or one's trials on the soccer field during military service.

편리하게 이용하고 죄책감 없이 버릴 수 있는 순수한 판타지를, 인간이 아닌 무언가를.

처음에는 디즈니풍 해피엔딩은 아니더라도(기저귀와 아이가 흘려놓은 밥풀들로 발 디딜 틈 없는 이런 세계에 낭만적인 감정이 들어설 수 있을까? 나는 아니라고 생각했다), '나'와 대니가 가까워진 뒤 모종의 사건을 함께 해결하거나, 즐거운 모험에 휘말렸다가 담백하게 마주보고 웃으며 끝나는 이야기 같은 걸 쓰려고 했다. 그런데 결국 이런 이야기가 되어버렸다. 왜일까.

어떤 기쁨도 고통만큼 나를 세상에 단단히 연결시켜 주지는 않는다.

현실을 살아가는 일만큼이나 환상을 만들어내는 일에도 책임이 따른다.

그리고 이유는 알 수 없지만, 쓰는 행위는 내게 종종, 내가 죽여버린 누군가를 기억하는 행위의 동의어다.

이 문장들이 혹시 대답이 될 수 있을까. 그랬으면 좋겠다.

Still, I wanted to invent something for these long-suffering women and offer them a present. Something that would restore them to their humanity, even for a moment, a pure fantasy that they could conveniently use and throw away without guilt, something non-human.

At first, I also wanted to write a happy ending, even if it couldn't necessarily be a Disney-style ending (Can romantic feelings enter into a world of diapers and discarded, strewn rice grains? I think not). But perhaps an ending where the narrator and Danny, after becoming friends, solve a mysterious event together. Or where they could smile innocently at each other after having a merry adventure. But, ultimately, the story ended the way it did. I wonder why.

No happiness connects me to the world as securely as pain does.

There is a responsibility in creating fantasy as much as in living in reality.

Although I don't know why, the act of writing is often synonymous with the act of remembering someone I killed within me.

By any chance, could my sentences be an answer? I hope so.

해설
Commentary

울지 마, 인조엄마

정은경 (문학평론가)

윤이형의 SF적 상상력은 욕망의 투영이기도 하고, 현실에 대한 절망이자 위로이며 격려이다. 자연은 주어진 그대로 완전한 게 아니라 결핍과 불완전을 내장한 '욕망'의 매개이므로, 작가는 '거짓말'과 '환상'의 픽션에서 백일몽을 펼쳐놓기도 한다. 윤이형이 「대니」에서 문제삼는 '자연'이란 '엄마'라는 보편적 존재인 동시에 한편 21세기 한국 엄마들의 '현실'이기도 하다.

「대니」의 화자는 72살의 할머니이다. 올드타운에서 혼자 사는 그녀는 유유자적 시장을 구경하고 산책을 하고 바자회에 다니고, 노인복지센터에서 마련해준 일을 소일거리 삼아 하면서 살아왔으나, 복직해야 하는 딸의

Don't Cry, Artificial Mom!

Jung Eun-kyoung (literary critic)

Yun I-hyeong's science-fiction story centers around the despair, as well as the solace and encouragement, of a particular reality, even as it also reflects a greater fantasy, a reflection of certain desires. Nature is not perfect. It is a medium of "desire" that contains deficiencies and imperfections. Yun presents a fictional dreamscape of lies and fantasy. In "Danny" Nature is the universal figure for the mother and the 21st-century Korean mother's reality.

The narrator of Yun's story is a 72-year-old grandmother. She lives alone, strolling leisurely in the marketplace, taking walks and visiting bazaars, and spending time working at jobs offered by the

청을 거절하지 못하고 6개월 된 아기를 맡게 된다. 아이를 보는 일은 엄마와 마찬가지로 할머니에게도 행복한, 고역이다. 그녀에게 손주는 "밤새 쌓인 첫눈" 같고, "세상에 하나뿐인 보석들만 모아 정성껏 세공해서 만든 귀한 그릇" 같이 예쁘지만, 그 아이를 돌보는 일은 "그 빛나는 그릇에 매일같이 담기는 타는 듯이 뜨겁고 검은 약을 남기지 않고 받아마시는 것"과 같은 일이다.

그녀는 새벽 6시부터 자정까지 종일 서서 생각할 겨를도 없이 반사적으로 몸을 움직여야 하고, 혼자 만의 시간은 엄두도 낼 수 없을 뿐 아니라, 때로 "돌고래처럼 악을 쓰고 발을 구르는" 아이를 감당해한다. 그런 전쟁 같은 시간으로 인해 그녀는 자신이 "그저 기름 약간 거죽 약간을 발라 놓은 뼈 무더기"와 같은 기계로 전락했음을 깨닫는다. "나는 기계가 아니다""차라리 기계라면 좋겠다"라는 그녀의 절규는 돌보미형 로봇인 안드로이드 베이비시터(AB)를 호출한다.

일명 '대니'라 불리는 스물 네 살의 돌보미형 로봇은 스물 네 살의 건장한 청년으로, 마흔 두 명의 아이들과 교사 여덟 명이 목숨을 잃은 킨더가든 참사로 탄생한 것으로 설정된다. 국가는 대책위원회를 꾸려 미국에서

elderly welfare center. She does all this until she has to take on the task of raising a six-month-old grandson for her daughter who must return to work. Taking care of the child is as happy yet difficult a task for her as it is for her daughter, the child's mother. To this narrator, the baby is "like the first snow that fell and accumulated overnight" and "like a precious, gem-studded bowl with each gem carefully, individually chosen." But the work of taking care of it is like "drinking up the hot and black herb tea that fill[s] that bowl every day."

She has to work nonstop on her feet and constantly remain on the move, unable to think quietly from six in the morning until midnight. She cannot even consider the notion of alone time, often having to deal with the baby "piping and squealing like a dolphin." Eventually the travails of her new duties bring her to the realization that she has become a sort of "heap of old bones covered over with a few drops of oil and a several patches of skin." She eventually cries, "I'm not a machine" and "I... wish I were a machine," calling attention to the idea of an Android Babysitter (AB), a caretaker robot that brings the story to its main focus.

This caretaker-type robot, Danny, as he is simply referred to, is a strong 24-year-old young male,

만들어진 이 로봇을 개조해 50개의 가정에 시범적으로 제공한다. 기계로 된 뇌와 튼튼한 팔다리를 가진 예쁘장한 청년 '대니'는 인간처럼 지치거나 짜증을 느끼거나 침울해하지 않을 뿐 아니라, 아이의 요구를 정확히 파악하여 대처하도록 설계되어 있다. 무엇보다 '대니'는 사람이라면 누구나 지닌 '불안정한 감정'이 없어 아이에게 절대적 안정과 돌봄을 제공할 수 있는 '완전한 엄마'가 될 수 있는 것이다.

「대니」는 물론 '엄마'의 '완전체'에 대한 일종의 판타지로서 한편, '엄마'라는 존재와 이를 대신하는 우리 시대의 '할머니'에 대한 작가의 실존적 성찰을 보여준다. 튼튼한 육체와 지치지 않는 마음을 가진 '대니'란 다름아닌 모든 엄마들의 이름이다. '엄마'는 24시간 전적으로 아이를 위해 존재하지만, 그 '엄마'는 '엄마' 이외의 존재를 기억하고 있는 인간이기도 하다. 관계맺기에 서툰 '나'는 타인과 단절된 채, 하고 싶은 말이 있으면 "화, 목, 일요일에 음식물 쓰레기와 함께 배출"하며 살아간다. 또한 '나'는 집이 비는 주말이면 소주를 마시며 "혼자만의 시간도 주기적으로 넣어줘야한다"며 사람이라는 더 높은 존재로의 회복을 꿈꾼다. 사람이 아닌 '기계인간'

born in the aftermath of a care-taking disaster in which 42 kindergarten children and eight teachers have died. Following the public outcry and anxiety after this catastrophe, Danny is the outcome of a government committee's decision to build and distribute this U.S.-made robot among 50 Korean families. An attractive young man with a mechanical brain and strong limbs, Danny does not get tired, annoyed, or depressed. He is designed to accurately measure and take care of children's needs. And, above all, Danny does not have the insecurities of human beings; he is a perfect mother who can offer absolute security and care for children.

"Danny" is a "perfect mom" fantasy; yet he is also a vehicle for the author's existential reflections on mothers and, in particular, grandmothers, who must assume the role of primary caregiver for their grandchildren in Korea in our age. "Danny," with his unwearying body and inexhaustible heart, represents the universal ideal of motherhood. This "mom" exists entirely for his children, performing his duties 24/7, and yet remains a human being who recognizes human needs that predate his or her motherhood.

But the grandmother-narrator, who is not very social by nature, collects her thoughts and

으로서의 엄마는 일종의 '아이'에게 봉쇄된 수도원에 갇힌 수녀인 셈이다. 이렇듯 고된 노동과 고독에 짓눌린 '나'에게 '대니'와의 만남은 '사람'으로의 회복을 의미한다. 놀이터에서 처음 만난 대니가 '나'에게 건넨 말은 '아름다워'이다. '나'에게서 노동하는 기계 이상의 것을 읽어낸 '대니'에게 이끌려 '나'는 그와 친구가 되고, 대니의 젊음과 유능함을 통해 '나'는 위안을 얻는다. 결정적으로 딸과 사위가 태국 여행을 떠난 동안 손자가 입원하여 속수무책일 때, 대니는 이런 '나'를 돌보기도 한다. 함께 장을 보기도 하고, 아이들을 돌보면서 대니는 '함께 사는 집'을 꿈꾸고, 천만원이 있으면 집을 빌릴 수 있다는 '나'의 말에 대니는 사람들에게 돈을 빌리기 시작한다. 그러나 이 기계의 '발칙한 꿈'은 결국 경찰에 의해 체포됨으로써 폐기되고 만다. 물론, '대니'도 그 꿈과 함께 폐기처분된다.

소외된 엄마들의 연대와 '인조엄마'의 판타지는 이렇게 파국을 맞지만, 이것이 곧 기계엄마의 가능성에 대한 실패를 의미하는 것은 아니다. 「대니」의 SF적 상상력은 기계엄마의 불가능성이 아닌, 기계와 다름없이 살아가는 모든 엄마들과 할머니에게 보내는 위로이자 격려

"[throws] them out every Tuesday, Thursday, and Sunday together with the garbage." She drinks *soju* alone on weekends and dreams of regaining her higher status as a "human being," an individual afforded the simple need of "regularly provided alone time." Thus, the mother as a "mechanical human being," a non-human type figure, is a sort of nun imprisoned in a convent of children.

In the narrator's cell of hard labor and loneliness, her meeting with Danny means a recovery of this essential humanity. Tellingly, the first word Danny says to her on the playground is "beautiful." The narrator becomes friends with Danny, who sees in her more than a toiling machine, and she regains a sense of security and comfort through his youth and competence. Critically, it is Danny who takes care of her when she endures a particularly difficult time due to her grandson's severe illness and hospitalization, while her daughter and son-in-law enjoy a weeklong vacation in Thailand. While shopping and taking care of the children alongside the narrator, Danny dreams of "living together" with the narrator and begins to borrow money from people after learning that they would need 10 million *won* to rent a house. Danny's impudent dreams, however, are frustrated when the police arrest him,

이다. 그 위로와 격려는 대니가 처음 '나'에게 건넨 '아름다워'라는 말에 담겨 있다. 이 아름다움의 수사는 "행복한 순간에도 견딜 때가 있었고, 견디는 순간에도 맛있는 음식을 먹는 것 같은 표정일 때가 있어요"라는 대니의 말처럼, 인간이라는 한계를 지녔으나 엄마라는 이름으로 끊임없이 그 한계를 넘어서야 하는 모든 엄마들에게 보내는 찬사인 것이다.

정은경 문학평론가. 1969년 서울에서 태어나고 고려대 독문과와 국문과 대학원을 졸업했다. 2003년 《세계일보》에 평론 「웃음과 망각의 수사학」으로 등단하였으며, 현재 아시아 문학전문 바이링궐 계간지 《아시아》의 편집위원으로 활동하고 있다. 2005년 고려대학교에서 「한국 근대소설에 나타난 악의 표상」으로 문학박사학위를 취득했으며, 현재 원광대 교수로 재직 중이다. 저서로 『디아스포라 문학』 『한국 근대소설에 나타난 惡의 표상 연구』 『지도의 암실』 등이 있다.

and Danny is thrown away together with his dream.

Although solidarity between the fantasy of the alienated and artificial mothers ends in catastrophe, this does not mean that the possibility of the artificial mom is abandoned. The sci-fi vision of "Danny" is not about the impossibility of the mechanical mother, but about offering a small sense of solace and encouragement for the mothers and grandmothers in the world who must live as if they were machines. Danny's first word to grandma, "beautiful," encapsulates this message of comfort and support. Danny notes in the story's conclusion, "[E]ven when she [Grandma] was enduring, she had an expression like she was eating something delicious." This story is a tribute to all women who continue to overcome their human limits in service to the eternal figure of the mother.

Jung Eun-kyoung Born in Seoul in 1969, Jung Eun-kyoung graduated from Korea university after majoring in German and Korean literature. She made her literary debut by winning *the Segye Ilbo* Spring Literary Competition in criticism with the article "A Rhetoric of Laughter and Forgetting: on Song Sok-ze." Her published works include *Literature of Diaspora, A Study of the Representation of Evil in Modern Korean Novels*, and *A Darkroom of Map*. She is currently a professor at the Division of Korean Language and Literature at Wonkwang University and a member of the editorial board of the magazine of Asian literature *ASIA*.

비평의 목소리
Critical Acclaim

윤이형이 보여주는 첨예한 문제의식과 성찰적 서사
의식이야말로 한국 단편소설의 특이성을 용감하게 증
언하고 있다.

「제5회 문지문학상 심사평」, 2015

때론 잔혹하고 때론 엽기적인 윤이형의 소설 속에서
반짝 이렇게 달팽이의 속살 같은 문장을 발견할 때가
나는 좋다.

하성란, 「제5회 젊은작가상 심사평」, 《문학동네》, 문학동네, 2014

More than any other author, Yun I-hyeong's acute critical eye and contemplative narrative awareness bravely testify to the special characteristics of Korean short stories.

"Judges' Remarks for the 5th Moonji Literary Award," 2015

I love the brilliant moments when I encounter sentences that feel like the inside meat of a snail in Yun I-hyeong's sometimes cruel and at other times grotesque short stories.

Ha Seong-nan, "A Judge's Remark for the 5th Young Writer Award," *Munhak dongne* 2014.

K-픽션 007
대니

2015년 4월 17일 초판 1쇄 발행

지은이 윤이형 | 옮긴이 전승희 | 펴낸이 김재범
기획위원 정은경, 전성태, 이경재
편집 정수인, 윤단비, 김형욱 | 관리 박신영
펴낸곳 (주)아시아 | 출판등록 2006년 1월 27일 제406-2006-000004호
주소 서울특별시 동작구 서달로 161-1(흑석동 100-16)
전화 02.821.5055 | 팩스 02.821.5057 | 홈페이지 www.bookasia.org
ISBN 979-11-5662-115-7(set) | 979-11-5662-117-1 (04810)
값은 뒤표지에 있습니다.

K-Fiction 007
Danny

Written by Yun I-hyeong I **Translated by** Jeon Seung-hee
Published by ASIA Publishers I 161-1, Seodal-ro, Dongjak-gu, Seoul, Korea
Homepage Address www.bookasia.org I **Tel**. (822).821.5055 I **Fax**. (822).821.5057
First published in Korea by ASIA Publishers 2015
ISBN 979-11-5662-115-7(set) | 979-11-5662-117-1 (04810)

금기와 욕망 Taboo and Desire

바이링궐 에디션 한국 대표 소설 set 6

운명 Fate

미의 사제들 Aesthetic Priests

식민지의 벌거벗은 자들 The Naked in the Colony

바이링궐 에디션 한국 대표 소설 set 7

백치가 된 식민지 지식인 Colonial Intellectuals Turned "Idiots"